Flawless Foolishness

Delia Rouse

Desired Reads Publishing
P.O. Box 575
Knightdale, N.C. 27545

First paperback edition September 2022
Library of Congress Control Number: 2022914512

ISBN 979-8-9867252-0-8
www.Deliarouse.com

DEDICATION

This is dedicated to my mother Paulette Nelson. I love her for doing what needed to be done, the best way she knew how to do it, in order to produce the best possible outcome in raising me. She will always be my favorite lady.

ACKNOWLEDGMENTS

Thank you, God. Thank you for the breath in my body and thank you for blessing me with my writing talent. To my husband Darrell and my kids Treasure and Kennedy thank you. Thank you for allowing me the space to write for hours on end and offering your thoughts and perspective with this story.

To Nicole Newman who has been instrumental in my writing journey, I love and appreciate you. To my mentor T. Styles, thank you for always answering my questions and taking the time out to teach me everything you know about the writing business, you, Charisse, and the Elite Writers Squad are nothing but love and light. To Erin Conigliaro, who provided love, support, and her creative talents and who believed in me from the very beginning. To her husband Sal who supported her while she supported me, you guys are the kindest couple I've ever experienced, and I am grateful that our daughters allowed us to cross paths and build a friendship.

Thank you to my Dreamers. Thank you for your love and your support. Thank you for sharing my love of reading and writing and for referring my books to others. Thank you for speaking my name. Thank you for sharing your dreams with me and allowing me to share mine with you. I'm forever grateful.

Flawless Foolishness

Delia Rouse

Desired Reads
PUBLISHING

Chapter One

S antino Wellington was a mystery to me. He texted me twice a month but called even less. My birthday was coming, and it reminded me he was an absent dad. The birth of a child was the result of two people connecting, but I only knew one of them. There was no baby father drama, no child support drama, no visitation drama, nothing. His fatherhood was just unaccounted for.

My mother didn't seem phased that I lacked that family tie and appeared like it pained her to speak of him, so I avoided bringing him up. I hadn't seen him in years and besides a picture sent every blue moon, he was a ghost to me. My dad's family was an enigma as well. I knew his parents were still alive, and he had three brothers who also had families.

My dad was more of a figment of my imagination; a man who threw himself into his new family, forgetting about his original family. His casual text message this morning put me in a bad mood. I deleted his message from my iPad and continued looking at a pair of sneakers I planned on asking my mom to buy for me.

"Ma, why do you always burst into my room without knocking? Dag, I have no privacy."

"Nina, I do not have to knock this is my home where I pay the bills." A vanilla and lavender fragrance entered with my mom.

I rolled my eyes and looked up at the chandelier. I was laying across my queen size bed with one ear pod in my ear while strolling on my tablet.

"That's unfair, Ma, children are people too," I responded while turning onto my stomach. My legs dangled off my bed and I was swinging them up and down like I was swimming.

"Get up and get ready. We have forty minutes until the party."

"I have nothing to wear," I said, still strolling on my tablet without looking up at my mother.

"Nina, you have a closet full of clothes. I just took you shopping last week!"

"I don't want to wear any of that."

"Nina." My mother took my tablet out of my hands.

"Please put on something so we can go. I don't want to be too late. We have a thirty-minute ride, so we need to be leaving in about twenty minutes." My mom sat my tablet on my nightstand.

"I'm not going." I reached over and picked my tablet back up.

"You will go."

"I don't want to go, Ma. These are your friends. I don't want to meet their daughter; we have nothing in common and we don't even speak in school. I don't feel like I should be made to go."

"Everything is not always about what Nina wants."

"If my attendance was so important, why didn't you buy me something new to wear?" I jumped up from my bed and walked casually toward my room door.

"Nina, pick something out of that two hundred- and sixty-three-dollars' worth of clothing that I purchased last week and be ready to go in twenty minutes."

I stood there with my hand on the doorknob and smiled. "Whatever, Mom, can you leave out of my room so I can have some privacy? If I go, I'm telling you now, I'm not going to be talking to her like we're friends. The only reason why I'm going to this party is because you are forcing me to. It is not my fault that she's new and can't make any friends."

"Nina that's unkind. I know I raised you better than this. Don't make me come back up here to get you." She pointed her finger in my face. I took her hand and kissed it while escorting her out of my room. She walked down the hall while shaking her head, and passed my nanny, Ms. Alba.

"Esa chica esta malcriada," she said, rolling her eyes.

"I love you too, Mom and I'm not spoiled!" I yelled down the hall. Ms. Alba smiled and shook her head, walking into my room with three sets of fresh towels.

"Ms. Alba, I hate when she makes me do things I don't want to do."

"I know, mi amor, but that's your mama and sometimes we have to just do it, okay. You'll probably have a great time. Stop arguing with your mama and have a great time."

She grabbed my chin with her soft hands and kissed my cheek while her floral scented perfume danced in my nostrils.

Me and my mom rode in silence. I was slouched down with my arms across my chest and stared into the open road. I could have been on the phone facetiming with my volleyball friends, but instead I was going with my mom to her co-worker's house to meet a new girl and help her transition into my school.

"Nina," my mom said sharply, snapping me out of my trance. "Make sure you're friendly tonight, introduce yourself to Tamia, and when you get to school on Monday introduce her to some of the other kids you know. You're very popular in school so it would be very important to me that you go ahead and make her feel welcomed."

"Since when is it my job to be the school's welcoming committee for Tamia? Nobody likes her because she's weird. I don't want to be seen with her because I don't want people to think I'm weird," I said, turning my head toward her.

"Nina, no one is going to think you are weird. It's hard being new in a setting where cliques are already formed. When my family moved here from Ghana, I was young, and no one wanted to be my friend. My accent was thick which made it worse. I wish someone would've befriended me. I was very lonely."

My mom barely got the word lonely out. Her voice lowered to the point it was hard to hear her. Her eyes glazed like she was having a painful flashback. My mother was one of the most beautiful women I had ever seen, and I couldn't imagine anyone not wanting to be friends with her. She had honey brown highlights in her short natural hair, blending nicely with her lightly speckled greys that littered her hairline. It was tapered to perfection while showing off her long, slender neck. My mother was 5'9" barefoot and I could count on my hands how many times I'd seen her in flats. Her skin was a smooth milk chocolate, and her body never revealed the aftermath of giving birth; she was a size eight.

"I'm not trying to be mean, Mommy, honestly. I'm sure she's a nice girl but I don't see how she has become my problem."

"Nina, don't upset me. Be nice, be friendly and be on your best behavior." My mom's large, almond shaped eyes darkened, and her wide nose flared, which was my cue to stand down. I shut my mouth and focused on the brick house we pulled up to. The massive windows didn't have any curtains and I could see people inside mingling. I dragged behind my mom slowly with my arms crossed in front of my denim jumpsuit, walking up to the door. We rang the bell and opening the door was a tall caramel boy.

"Hello, my name is Chuck. I'm the Collins' oldest son. Welcome to our home, my parents are in the living room with the rest of the guest. Please come in."

"Hello, Chuck, it's so good to finally meet you. I heard so many great things about you and how you're excelling in college." My mom hugged him and then stepped to the side.

My name is Omalara, everyone calls me Ola, and this is my daughter Santina, but everyone calls her Nina."

Yummy, a college boy.

I dropped my arms so Chuck could see my full 36 C's. I decided to follow my mother's lead and gave him a hug. Instead of the side hug my mom gave, I did a front hug, pressing my boobs into his firm chest.

"Nice to meet you both. I'll take you in the basement with the rest of the teenagers so the adults can do their thing."

Wow, I'm glad I did come. I wished I spent more time picking a hot outfit. Chuck was fine. I had no idea Tamia had an older brother in college. I thought her weird ass was an only child.

I recognized a few faces once I was in the basement. Tamia was in the corner looking down and fidgeting with her hair.

"Hey Tamia," I said enthusiastically, not because I wanted to get to know her but because I wanted to get to know her brother.

"Hey Nina!" Tamia eyebrows raised and she smiled.

"Oh wow! I can't believe you're at my house. I saw you play in the volleyball game against August Martin High School last night; you were amazing." Tamia was talking fast. Her light skin was flushed on her cheeks and a small chunk of spit flew out of her mouth. I couldn't get in a word.

"I sure wish I could play volleyball like you! I wanted to try out for the team next year since I transferred in too late to make tryouts this year." Tamia must've run out of air because she finally paused, allowing me to speak.

"Well, I train a lot which is why I'm a fourteen-year-old freshman on varsity and it takes a long time to get as good as me but keep practicing. Our school is division one in athletics so making the team will be hard." I searched for her brother in the dimly lit basement.

Tamia touched my arm, forcing me to redirect my attention toward her.

"Do you think you could work with me so that I can be ready for next year?"

"Nah, I don't have time, but I'm sure your parents can find someone to train you. I also play club volleyball and travel most weekends. Practicing, homework, and games take up most of my time."

I was ready to dismiss Tamia. "What school does your brother go to?" I blurted out.

"He goes to Lincoln."

"How often does he come home?"

"Not much because he is in a lot of clubs and his fraternity keeps him busy. When his school semester is out, he stays in Pennsylvania since he has an off-campus apartment. He's only home to help us get settled. He leaves next week to go back to PA."

I wrinkled my nose and blew air through my mouth. *That sucks,* I thought.

"Okay, well, let me mingle and I will talk to you a little later." I touched Tamia's arm and turned around straining my neck to find Chuck in the small crowd.

I had no intentions of making my way back to Tamia. She proved to be clingy already, and I didn't want her to attach herself to me when we got back to school. Her skin was broken out and braces protruded from her mouth. It was not a good look.

I walked around the basement and found Chuck with a few of his friends standing by a pool table. They were talking with a couple of girls. It was three guys and three girls, and they looked like they were coupled up.

"Hey guys," I said, waving my hand while approaching the group slowly.

"Hey Nina." Chuck waved back then gave me the hand motion to come over. "These are some of my friends visiting from our old neighborhood. Guys this is Nina...Nina goes to high school with Tamia."

"Hey Nina," they said with a lackluster response in unison. The girls looked me up and down like I was trash. The boys were looking at me like I was a kid. One even patted my arm like I was a toddler.

"High school, huh? We remember those days." Everyone laughed except me. I turned around without a word and walked upstairs to find my mother.

"Ma," I said, interrupting her conversation with Mrs. Collins and another woman whose perfume was too strong and made me sneeze. "I don't feel well, Ma. I want to go home."

"Excuse me," my mom said politely, walking me toward the corner of the room.

"Nina, what's wrong?"

"I said I don't feel well." My tone was sharp. "Can we go home now? I came to this party. I introduced myself to Tamia like you asked and now I am ready to go." My hand was on my hip.

"Nina, what the hell is your problem?" my mom asked in a harsh whisper. "I ask you to sacrifice one evening and do this one thing and you're acting like I asked you to give up an arm. We are not leaving. Now take your behind where the other kids are and mingle until I'm ready to go."

"Okay," I said, tilting my head to the side and squinting my eyes. I walked into the dining area where all the food was set up.

I piled a smorgasbord of food on my plate then sat in the corner. I ate and ate until I was stuffed. I looked around at everyone in the dining room and they were in deep conversations. I turned my head toward the wall and stuck my finger in my mouth. I felt the throw up rising, ran to the edge of the doorway that looked out into the party, and I threw up on the floor.

"Oh goodness!" someone yelled.

"Ola, come here quick. Your daughter is sick!" Mr. Collins screamed.

Blargh

I was dry heaving while holding my stomach. I was on my knees while globs of spit suspended three inches from my mouth to the floor. The hostess grabbed a towel and came over to help me.

"Nina! Nina! are you okay, honey?" my mom yelled, running to me. She bent down and rubbed my back.

I saw a gentleman in the corner trying to hold his hand over his mouth. It didn't work and he threw up too.

BLARGH

A sour smell filled the room and his vomit splattered all over his shoes and on his wife's red silk dress. Another person got sick, and it created a shit storm of the nastiest chain reaction I had ever seen. I raised my head and reached for my mom. I looked at her with sorrowful tear-filled eyes.

"Mommy, my stomach is hurting so bad. I feel so sick," I whined.

"I am so sorry that you got sick, baby. It must have been something in the food which is why several of the guest are sick."

"Your stomach not hurting, Ma?" I clutched my stomach and doubled over.

"No, I hadn't eaten anything yet. I was running my mouth and chatting with Sofia, all I had was a glass of wine."

"Oh, well lucky you, Ma. Not only do I feel horrible, but I ruined my outfit."

"Don't worry about the outfit, Nina. Alba will get it cleaned. Worst case scenario, we can always buy you more clothes."

"Thanks, Ma. I'm so sorry I ruined your time at the party. I know you was looking forward to this."

I pivoted on my heels, looked down, and smirked while following my mother as she said swift goodbyes and rushed me home.

Chapter Two

"**N**ina! Please stop talking in my class. If my lesson plan is not pleasing to you then you can leave."

"Sorry, Mrs. Talston, I was answering a question that Tamia had. You know she's new to the school and I wanted to make sure that she understood what was going on."

"Oh okay. Well, thank you for helping her...try to be less disruptive next time."

Tamia froze and her eyes bulged. She hadn't asked me anything I was asking her questions about her brother.

BUZZZZ

Everyone jumped up and grabbed their backpacks. Grinning to myself, I was excited for our volleyball game. It was with our biggest rivals, and I was hoping to produce a win.

When I walked toward the locker, my friend Sidney stopped me.

"Hey, Nina."

"Hey, Sidney."

"Are you ready for the game today?"

"Yeah, I am ready."

"I hope so. I heard that you were sick this weekend and puked all over yourself at the Collins' house."

"Where did you hear that from?" My face tightened because no one from school was at the party so how did she know that?

"The new girl was telling us at lunch."

"Really?" My steps staggered a bit. I re-adjusted my heavy backpack. Placing all my weight on one leg, I cocked my head to the side and looked at Sidney. She was holding back a laugh with her lips tucked.

"Well, did she tell you that I got sick because there was a roach in the food?"

"What?" Sidney covered her mouth in disgust then screamed. "Ewwww!"

"Yes girl. The house was nice, but I think they have a roach infestation because I saw one when I went to the bathroom, and I saw one in the food. That's why I threw up. I don't have roaches and I only seen them on tv. It was disgusting."

"Oh my God! Tamia left that part out." Sidney rubbed her arms like she was itching.

"I bet she did." My jaws clenched. Tamia was new to the school and was already trying to embarrass me.

Walking into my coach's classroom, I sat down to do my homework. There was one hour and thirty minutes before the game started, and I had a load of homework to do.

"Hey, Nina." Our volleyball setter smiled, walking toward me.

"Hey, Shelby," I said. "You ready for today's game?"

"Yeah, I think so." I fidgeted with my bookbag zipper. I didn't want to show Shelby I was nervous about the game.

"Shelby, they are our toughest competition. We must be ready because you know that they will be ready for us. I need you to set my balls high. Last game, they were a little too low which didn't allow me to spike power balls like I wanted to."

"Okay. I got you."

"I hope so, Shelby. I really want to beat this team. I'm pissed that we lost to them last season. It's time that we redeem ourselves."

"True. I hate that school. I want to beat them too."

"Good, bring that energy into the game today. We are going to need it." I smiled at Shelby and opened my textbook when I heard someone calling my name.

"Nina!" Tamia was walking fast into the classroom toward me.

"Nina, why did you tell Sidney that I had roaches in my home. We do not have bugs. I have never had a roach in my home." Tamia's fists were balled at her sides.

"What are you talking about?" I shook my head and looked around. She was drawing a small crowd.

"You know what I am talking about! Why would you tell Sidney that shit?"

"I'm sorry, do I know you?" I asked with scrunched eyebrows while pretending to try to recognize her.

With bugged eyes, Tamia looked at me like she was in shock. My teammates were cracking up.
"Oh, so now you don't know me?" Tamia chest was rising and falling rapidly.
"Tell me your name again? It's Shonda, right?" I was still sitting, looking up at her with my hand on my chin.

"Tamia, bitch! You know my name." Tamia's acne laced face was red as she looked down on me.

"Why are you so angry? You only been here a couple of weeks and already you're bullying me?" I placed my hand over my chest. "What's your problem. All I'm trying to do is get my homework done. I have a volleyball game today. I am an athlete for this school. I do not want to fight. That's not how the Wild Cats represent our school." I bit my bottom lip and I looked back down at my textbook.

"What is all this ruckus? What is going on here?"

"Coach Simmons, I was trying to do my homework before our big game and this girl approached me accusing me of something I didn't even do. I do not even know why she's in here. I thought this was a safe space for the team?" My voice dropped and my eyes watered while talking to the coach.

"Yes, you do!" Tamia screamed. "You know me! You know damn well you know me!" Tamia was loud and she stomped her left foot.

"Hey. Hey. Hey, young lady," Coach Simmons said in an authoritative tone. She ushered Tamia with her pointer finger and snapped. "Come with me. You need to leave. This room is for my team to have quiet time and study before games. I don't care who you are, that is not the behavior we co-sign around here, young lady." Coach was pointing to the door.

Tamia was fuming. She looked around frantically at the audience she created. I smirked and a couple of students were recording her outburst. She lowered her eyes and muttered something as she sprinted out the door. Coach didn't play games. She was hard core and if she thought you were a threat to her team, she would remove you. Coach Simmons wanted to win the state championship by any means necessary, which meant making sure her players were in peak performance which meant getting Tamia's ass out of my face.

I changed into my uniform and tied my long twists up into a bun. My hair was natural and thick. I didn't like it down while I played ball. I lotioned my long, chocolate legs while tugging on my tiny volleyball shorts. My hips were wide, and my ass was muscular and semi flat which made me self-conscious since my cheeks often peeked out during games. I looked out the small classroom window into the gym and noticed that spectators were coming in already.

My team walked into the gymnasium and the crowd was massive. I could barely hear myself think because the cheers were thunderous. The other team walked in looking like they were on stilts.

"Damn...did the team grow from since the last time we played them?" I said out loud to no one in particular.

I warmed up and looked for my partner so we could start the team drills. Looking around the gym, I saw my mom and Ms. Alba walk in. They sat in their normal spots on the front row. Ms. Alba had been my nanny since I was small, and she was like a second mom to me. I was always happy to see her face in the crowd.

BUZZZZZ

It was now showtime.

"Wildcats! Wildcats! Wildcats!" was all I heard in the gym. I glanced to the left and saw Tamia in the stands with her brother. Locking eyes with Tamia, she threw up two middle fingers. I ignored her and got into my serve receive position so that I would be ready.

SMASH

"Oweeeee!" the crowd roared. I pretended the ball was Tamia's face and hit the ball so hard when Shelby set it to me; my opponent couldn't recover it.

"Serve, Pass, Kill," the crowd chanted this phrase non-stop. I killed the ball, scoring the point every time Shelby set me the ball. I looked over at Tamia every single time I got a kill. Eventually, she looked away or fumbled in her bag to my eye contact. She would learn. If I had anything to do with it, she would never play on this court with me. Coach called a time out.

"Okay, team. We only need two points. We are up by three and I think we can do it." The coach was sweating bullets as if she was on the court playing the game.

"We need a solid serve. We need good passes. Nina, we need a kill shot." The coach's pleading eyes made me feel pressured. I wiped my sweaty forehead with the back of my hand. I lifted my left foot and swiped my palm against the bottom of my sneaker. I lifted the bottom of my right foot and did the same.

"Our defense has to be top notch. Girls, you must remain strong at the net. Back row, I don't want any balls hitting the floor. Two points team. Play aggressively and play smart. We can do this!" she yelled, lifting her arms up inside of our circle. "Wild Cats on three. One two three," she screamed.

"WILD CATS!"

It was the moment of truth. Chanting and loud yells smothered the gym. The audience's stomps were thunderous.

Swat! Our opponents served the ball. A tall girl served the ball straight to me. The ball came at me fast and I hit the ball into the crowd. I saw several people duck.

"Damn!" I screamed, clinching my fist on the side of my head. I glanced in Tamia's direction, and she was smirking.

The team served the ball to me again. If a player didn't hit well the first time, they continued serving the ball to them.

I received this ball and hit it upward so hard, it hit the ceiling and came straight down over the referee's head. He extended his arm and blew the whistle, indicating the other team scored.

Shit! Tamia had gotten into my head.

"Nina, pass the damn ball like you know how to play or I will take you out!" my coach yelled.

I glanced at Tamia, and she was giggling, saying something in her brother's ear. He wasn't even that cute to me anymore. My teammate, Naomi, served the ball and scored with an ace; no one hit her ball. The crowd went wild. We still needed two more points. Naomi served the ball again and it went into play.

"Four! Four! Four!" I yelled, which meant to set the ball to the outside hitter—me.

I slapped the ball hard, but the team blocked it. I recovered the block and Shelby set it to Brittany and she got the kill. I was grateful although I wished my shot landed the power point.

The ball went into play after Naomi served again Shelby set me the ball and I jumped up as high as my Nikes would take me, floating in the air like a bird. I hit the ball like my life depended on it.

The ball landed into an empty hole. My opponent slid to pancake the ball but missed.

It was pandemonium in the gym.

"Nina! Nina! Nina! Nina!" my team screamed repeatedly.

Tamia stopped in her tracks and looked around the gym. I looked at her and nodded with just enough time before my team rushed me, yelling, and screaming. We won the game, and I got the winning point!

That would show her who's bossed up at this school. I hope she took mental notes. Tamia looked down and walked behind her brother out of the gym.

Delia Rouse

Chapter Three

"Wake up, Nina. Wake up, Baby!" Nina's mom rubbed her cheek.

"Hey, Mommy. I'm tired. I don't want to get up." I blinked rapidly, rubbing the crud from my eyes to focus.

"I know. I know, but look at what I got." She held up her arms and there were several brown wrapped boxes with thin red ribbons in different sizes along with shopping bags. My mom ran her tongue over her teeth and cracked a smile from ear to ear.

I sat up, rubbed my eyes, and smiled. "Ma, what is all of this?"

"Duh, it's early birthday gifts!"

Ms. Alba walked in with a breakfast tray.

"Happy- Birthday, Princess Nina."

"Happy Birthday to you! Happy Birthday to you. We love you to pieces and God loves you too!"

"Yay!" I squealed, throwing my arms in the air, freeing my lap for my birthday tray. I loved the twist Ms. Alba put on her version of the birthday song. She spoke broken English and her accent made it special.

"Thank you, Mommy. Thank you, Ms. Alba."

I looked down to see a plate of french toast with fresh blueberries and strawberries toppled over the brioche bread. Thick cut bacon and cheese and eggs laid beside it along with warm strawberry syrup and powdered sugar.

"Ms. Alba, this is my absolute favorite breakfast ever! Thank you so much."

"Anything for you, Princess Nina."

"Ma, my birthday is not until Thursday. I thought we would be celebrating next weekend. You surprised me by celebrating a week early."

"I know, honey. I wanted to celebrate early because I was just informed that I have to travel this week for work. There is a major delay with our distributors in Seattle and it is holding up a ton of important projects. We are in jeopardy of losing twelve million in revenue and I have to go see what's going on." My mom laid her right hand on my leg and rubbed it up and down to soften the blow.

"Ma, can't they send someone else? I hate your job. They always make you do everything. Don't they know you have a kid?"

"Honey, this job affords us this lifestyle. That walk-in closet full of clothes that you have and this house that we got custom built because you just had to have you a private bathroom and sitting area in your room is paid for because of that job your hate of mine." My mom swung her arm around her head in a grand gesture like she was Vanna White.

"I guess." I moved my shoulders up and down, then dug into my breakfast.

"Now, honey, don't be like that. Ms. Alba and I spent the last several days planning some fun things to do with you this weekend for your birthday."

"Ma, I don't want to do anything THIS weekend for my birthday because my birthday is NEXT weekend." I looked up with raised eyebrows.
"Santina Omalara Wellington. Are you being unappreciative? Cause I will take all these fabulous gifts and that tray of food from you." My mom stood up with her hands on her hips and threw a nod toward Alba.

"Alba, you should have fixed her a bowl of cereal."

"Maaaa, I'm just being honest. You shouldn't be traveling on my birthday while I am stuck here with Ms. Alba." I smiled and giggled. I heard a soft gasp and looked up. I noticed Ms. Alba's back stiffened. She didn't say anything, but I knew I'd hurt her feelings. I forgot she was in the room.

"No disrespect, Ms. Alba. I love spending time with you. I was kidding," I said in a low tone. I moved my eggs around a pool of syrup on my plate. I felt horrible for saying that because Ms. Alba helped my mom take good care of me.

"You know something, Nina. I do the best that I can around here. I'm a single mom and Ms. Alba has helped me with you since me and your dad split when you were four. I trust her with you before I trust your own dad with taking care of you. How dare you say something like that. Now you apologize to her right this second!"

My mother glared at me with her arms crossed, tapping her foot. She rarely got upset. She would go off on me when I went too far and this was one of those times.

"I am so sorry, Ms. Alba." I moved my tray carefully then jumped off my bed to reach down to hug her small frame. I squeezed her tight. "I love you so much and if I had to be with anyone other than my mom it would be you." I kissed her face and put my hands on her shoulders, looking into her eyes.

"Especially since you make the absolute best french toast and mac and cheese that I have ever had in my entire life." Ms. Alba laughed and rubbed my arm which was now around her neck.

"I know you didn't mean harm, Princess Nina. Every child prefers mama. That is normal but your mama must work, and I will take good care of you while she is away te prometo."

"I know, Ms. Alba. You always do."

"Yes, mi amor, and I always will."

My mom gathered my gift bags at the foot of my bed.

"Oh, Ma, you can pass those to me. I will open them now."
I reached in her direction.

"Oh no, no, no, honey. Do you think you deserve gifts after all that meanness you spewed? You will now wait until next week to get these gifts. I mean, if we are being honest here, today technically is not your birthday." With that, she walked out the door.

"Ma, wait!" I yelled, raising my hand up and running toward my bedroom door.

"I apologized to Ms. Alba. Can you at least leave one for me to open today? I see a LV shopping bag. Can I open that one?"
"No. However, you can clean your room, straighten up that closet, and scrub down your bathroom."
I furrowed my brow and looked at Ms. Alba. I was baffled. I hadn't cleaned my own room in forever.
"Huh?" I heard her, but I hoped she was joking.
"Yes, honey. You heard me. Ms. Alba is off this weekend. I have now decided that I would celebrate her and give her a break. You're on your own for the next couple of days so you better enjoy that yummy breakfast and make sure you wash the dishes up when you're done."

"What! Ma, my body is tired. I played a five-set match last night against our toughest competition. My legs are killing me, and my arm is sore from swinging. I was hoping to just relax today and soak in the hot tub."

"That sounds like a great idea. You can relax and soak. I'll pick you up some lavender salt for your bath. You can do all of that after you finish cleaning."

I closed my left eye while I scratched my scalp rigorously.

"I'm running out to pick up some last-minute things that I need before I catch my flight Monday morning." My mom still had all my gifts in her hands.

"What about the fun filled weekend we had planned?"

"You didn't want to do anything this weekend, remember? Next weekend is your birthday. Therefore, we will not do a thing.

I looked around my room and it was an absolute mess. My throw pillows from my love seat were all over the floor. My vanity had scattered nail polish bottles everywhere. A pungent smell came from my bathroom where my sweaty uniform and volleyball sneakers from the night before were the culprit. My mirror beamed sunrays across my room. I looked at my reflection in the large custom framed sketch that my mom and I created together, rolled my eyes, and shook my head.

Nina, you talk too fucking much!

Chapter Four

I leaned over to the driver's seat and pressed the horn on Ms. Alba's steering wheel. I enjoyed bugging her because nothing really fazed her.

"Nina, por favor detente," she said, swatting my hand playfully.

The worst part of my day was waiting in the carpool lane. It moved at a snail's pace and Ms. Alba drove slowly. That was one of the few things that irritated me about her. If the light was yellow, she stopped. She drove in silence and with both hands on the wheel like she was taking a driving test.

"Ms. Alba, if you let every single car and every single kid walk in front of us, we will never move up and I will never get into school."

"Patience, mi amor. I cannot hit a child and we have plenty of time before the bell rings. Cual es la prisa?"

"No rush. It's just feels like we have been in carpool forever. Not to mention, Ms. Alba, as much as I love you, I have to admit that you drive very slow."

"No, my dear, you like to drive rapida!"

Her thick accent and her tiny fingers pointed upward in the air made me laugh out loud.

"Mira, it is our turn to get out now."

"It's about time," I said dramatically, rolling my eyes. I kissed Ms. Alba on the cheek and grabbed my things.

"Ms. Alba, don't forget I have a game today at 5:30."

"I don't forget, Princess Nina."

"Okay and it's an away game at Claremont High so you will have to meet me there. I will ride the activity bus to the game, but I will have to ride home with you, okay?"

"Si. I will be there. You have a good day in school, okay."

"Yes, ma'am, I will."

I ran into the school building and made my way to my locker.

On my way to my physics class, I saw Tamia walking toward me on the opposite side of the hall. I braced myself for a run-in with her. I looked directly at her then stopped. She kept her head down and never looked up at me. I guess she got the message.

I chuckled to myself. I was still shocked at her flipping me double birds.

This day seemed like it lasted forever. I checked my phone, and I didn't have any missed calls or text from my mom. That was weird because she normally made sure she texted me good morning when she was away. I knew we had a three-hour time difference so I assumed she may not have gotten around to it.

"Santina Wellington please report to the principal's office. Santina Wellington please report to the principal's office right now. Thank you."

The loudspeaker blared and all eyes were on me in class. My physics' teacher, Mr. Holder, was writing on the white board. He looked over his shoulder and nodded at me, indicating that I could go.

It baffled me as to what the principal wanted with me. I had a bad feeling it was Tamia. I was sure she whined to her teacher that I intimidated her in the hallway by staring her down and now I would be 'talked to.' This new girl was becoming a pain in my side quickly.

I walked into the office and was ready to plead my case. Tamia was obsessed with me, and I had no idea why. That's what I planned on telling the staff.

When I got into the room Tamia was not there. It was the principal, the guidance counselor, and Ms. Alba.

I looked at Ms. Alba and her shoulders were trembling.

"What are you doing here? Is everything okay? Why are you crying, Ms. Alba? Are you hurt?"

I walked toward her. She broke down crying and unable to speak.

I was desperate for clarity, looking back and forth from the principal to the counselor. My stomach dropped and I felt nauseous instantly.

"Nina, have a seat, dear," the counselor said in a soft tone.

"I'm fine. I'll stand." I hugged Ms. Alba while she sobbed uncontrollably. I bent down to look into Ms. Alba's eyes.

"Ms. Alba, is everything okay with your family back in El Salvador?" I had her small, soft hands in mine, rubbing the top of them with my thumbs gently.

"Nina, I don't know how to tell you this. You may not have seen this news alert on your phone since you have been in class but there was a terrible workplace shooting at a plant in Seattle this morning. Twenty-six people are confirmed dead. Nina...I am sorry, but your mother was one of those people."

"I'm sorry. What? I think you're mistaken because my mom is traveling for work and she just went to talk to some people about some stuff being late. She is not an employee out there." I stood up, shaking my head, and speaking fast. My mind was racing.

"Nina," the counselor said, touching my arm.

I snatched it away violently. "Don't touch me. You guys are lying. You don't even know my mom."

"Princess Nina," Ms. Alba whispered.

"Yes." I turned swiftly and kneeled back down in front of her. "Yes, Ms. Alba," I stated again but louder.

"Are you going to tell me they are lying? Where's your phone? I left mine in my book bag in class. Where's your phone? Call my mom! Dial her right now, Ms. Alba!"

"Santina, your mama didn't make it. They called me today, which is why I came straight over to tell you." Ms. Alba's bloodshot eyes and pink nose told me she was telling the truth.

"Noooooooo! Noooooooo!" I yelled and screamed to the top of my lungs. I yelled so hard that my throat burned. Everything around me became blurry. The principal's mouth was moving but his voice was muffled. I couldn't hear anything he was saying. Two more people ran into the office. I couldn't make out who they were because my vision blurred. I wasn't sure if it was because of the tears or because I had started losing my bodily functions and maybe my sight was leaving me too. My legs weakened, and I couldn't stand. I collapsed onto the floor and my head felt heavy. There wasn't anything in focus and I slipped into an unconscious state, hoping that when I woke up my mother was standing in front of me telling me to clean my messy room.

Chapter Five

I was numb. My eyes burned a hole in the picture of our Savior that was hanging high in the front of the church. I wondered why churches loved stained glass as I watched the sun reflect through the high-colored stained-glass windows.

"So sorry for your loss, Nina."

"I am so sorry, Nina, for your loss."

"My condolences, Nina."

I hated those phrases. My body tensed every time a random person hugged me or placed their nasty lips on my cheek.

Who are all these people?

"God Bless you, Nina."

"We're here for you if you need anything."

Oh really? You weren't here for me when my mom was alive so I'm supposed to believe you would be here for me when I need you now that she's dead?

I felt like I was in a factory. Droves of people walked by, looked into my mother's casket, came and hugged me, mumbled something random, then walked away.

The ritual was robotic. The phrases were empty. It was things people were conditioned to say when someone died, and I hated being on the receiving end.

My uma grabbed my hand and applied gentle pressure. I missed my uma so much. Since she lived in Africa, I didn't get a chance to see her and my umpa that much.

On the other side of me was my father. I sat as far from him as the slender pew allowed, almost sitting in my uma's lap. Santino was tall with a slim build. Not overly muscular but toned and in shape. He had smooth, peanut colored skin and deep dimples like mine. He had a low haircut that showed pronounced waves with a gentle sprinkle of greys. His eyes were covered with black sunglasses, and he had on a black tailored suit.

I flinched when he patted my leg. *Wow, he's patting me like I'm a dog.*

On the opposite side of him was his half-white looking wife. I don't even know why Nicole came. She made it known over the years that she couldn't stand my mother.

"Nina, don't worry, honey. We will get through this together and I will always make sure you're good." My dad kissed my forehead. I wanted to wipe off his invisible lip stain.

Lying ass. How is he going to make sure I'm alright when he barely visited or called when my mother was alive.

I was stoic, staring straight ahead. The service was a blur. Two men in black suits came out of nowhere to conclude the service. They pivoted on their heels like robots with stiff arms and balled fist with their back to us.

I strained my head to the side because I could no longer see my mother's face.

"Are they covering her face with a white cloth?" I didn't want them to close my mother's casket.

I sobbed. I was frightened. I didn't have any family in the States. My grandparents lived in another country. I barely knew my father's parents. My mother was the only person that I had and the person I loved more than anyone in this world.

The men moved the white, satin cloth that lined the outside of the casket and began to tuck it neatly.

"Noooo! Don't close my mother's casket!" I screamed, startling the men. They looked at me over their shoulders then they looked at each other. I extended my arms with my palms facing the men. I was now sitting on the edge of the front pew. The men froze. My dad nodded at them to stop and step to the side.

My dad grabbed me while giving me cheek to cheek contact with his face. My uma broke down in blood curdling screams while my umpa sat with wide legs and his head in between his hands.

"Me do wo Ola, Me do wo." My umpa kept proclaiming his love for his daughter.

"Mommy! Mommy!" I couldn't stop screaming for her.

"She's gone, baby. Your mom is in heaven now. I got you, baby, and I will take good care of you."

"No! No! No! No! I want my mama. I want my mama!" The pressure in my head made my eyes throb.

"I know, baby. I know you do," my dad said in a very low and shaky voice.

"I want her too. Here. Look."

He reached into his suit jacket and pulled out a small picture. It was of the three of us. I looked like I was two or three years old.

I was sitting in my dad's lap and my mom was smiling and leaning her head against his face. Her right arm was stretched across my lower abdomen and her hand touched his waist. It looked like she was trying to hug both of us with one arm. We looked happy.

"Let's go place this inside of Mommy's casket so that we will always be with her, okay. Would you like to do that?"

"Yes," I said through my snivels.

My dad walked me toward my beautiful mother slowly. She laid in the rose gold casket, looking angelic with a cream dress on. Her milk chocolate skin was perfect. Her short thick hair was adorned with a sparkly crystal rhinestone headpiece. It made her look regal.

"I will always love you, Omalara Folade Ayinde," my dad said quietly, kissing my mother's forehead and placing the picture under her folded hands.

He snuggled me closer to him and rubbed my shoulder while we stared at my mother.

"Your mother is the most beautiful woman I have ever known. She had a heart of gold and loved you more than anything or anyone in this world. You were made from love, our love. I loved her deeply and she will always be with you, Santina. Always remember that her spirit lives within you." I looked at my dad and tears streamed like a river onto his suit jacket. He took out his handkerchief and wiped his face and nose.

"Okay," I said, shaking my head up and down, while trying to hold back screams that wanted to burst out of me like a pressure cooker whistling.

"I will always love you too, Mommy." I looked down into the casket with the heaviest heart I had ever experienced. My dad flipped his hankie on the back side and wiped my tears.

"You want to kiss Mommy goodbye?"

"Yes." I was shaking.

"You can gently kiss her."

My dad held my waist, and I gripped his arm. I wasn't sure if I thought I would fall into the casket. My nose was running like a faucet, so I used the sleeve of my dress to wipe it. I muffled a piercing scream into the crook of my arm and felt my dad kiss the side of my face.

"It's okay," I heard him say.

I leaned over to kiss her cheek but flinched. I didn't expect her face to be ice cold. I'd never kissed a corpse before.

As we walked back to our seats, my dad nodded to the funeral director, and they proceeded to close my mother's casket. I stopped and turned around to watch their every move.

They slid a massive spread of white roses from the bottom of the casket toward the top. As I continued walking back to my seat, my stepmother sat rigid like a statue. Her massive, black shades hid her facial expression and her lace covered hands were folded neatly over her snakeskin purse.

God help me if I have to live with her.

Chapter Six

People filled the cream-colored round tables, chattering and eating. There was a bouquet of flowers in the center of each table. The clacking of the forks on the ceramic plates annoyed me. I observed how in less than an hour after my mother's service everyone moved on as if nothing happened. I wanted to wipe the smiles and joy off everyone's faces.

"Nina, we made this for you." My teammates and coach snapped me from my thoughts.

"Thank you, Shelby. Thank you, guys." They enveloped me in a massive group hug. I was happy to see them. So many of my classmates and several of my teachers came to support me.

"Guys, please stay and have some food. There's plenty," I stated weakly. I felt exhausted and my eyes were sore from crying.

"We have to run, Nina. I got to get the kids back to the school. We just wanted to say we love you and we are thinking of you, and you call us if you need to talk or if you need anything," my coach said in a soft tone I wasn't used to. She was normally stern and loud.

"Thank you." I could see my dad approaching out the corner of my eye.

"Hello, I am Santino. Nina's dad." He extended his hand to my teammates. They smiled and stared. Most of them didn't even know I had a dad since he was never around. It was always me, my mom, and Ms. Alba.

My dad shook every single one of my classmates and teachers' hands. He acted like such a proud dad, but it baffled me because where was this behavior during my award ceremonies, graduations, and championship games? I understood that he lived out of state, but he never tried to attend anything, not even once a year.

"Everybody this is Ms. Alba. She has been my nanny since I was four." It was important to introduce Ms. Alba. I didn't want her to feel left out. She was my true family.

"We know her," my coach said, smiling. "Ms. Alba is a familiar face on the front row of every game." She gave Ms. Alba a warm hug.

There was a harsh clicking of heels against the hardwood floors that broke up the warm and fuzzies. My stepmother burst into the group like an intruder and stood eye to eye with my dad with her four-inch stilettos on.

"Hello, everyone my name is Nicole. I am Nina's other mother." She extended her arm toward my coach. I felt my insides explode. Before I could speak up, my dad interjected. He must've felt the heat rising from me.

"Forgive me for being rude. This is my wife, Nicole. This is Nina's stepmother." Perplexed by her diva behavior, my friends gave her a lack luster hello and only one person took her hand and shook it.

I said my goodbyes to my classmates then walked away.

"Uma, what will happen to me?" I sat near her in the dining hall curious to know if I would be yanked out of my school mid-year, leaving all my friends. My stomach was in knots.

"Do they speak English in Africa, Umpa?" I asked, unsure if I was staying with Ms. Alba, my dad, or moving to another country. I had only visited Africa twice and the first time I was too young to remember.

"Aane, they speak English in our town, honey. You will be fine," my umpa responded while rubbing my back.

"Ms. Alba, can I just stay with you?" I turned my head swiftly toward her. Ms. Alba looked at me with watery eyes.

"I wish, Princess Nina, but that is not my decision. We will talk about that later but for now, come por favor try to eat something." Ms. Alba pushed the baked macaroni and cheese, oxtails in gravy, and green beans in front of me. Under different circumstances, I would've devoured my plate. It was impossible today. I had a million things running through my mind and eating was the last thing that I wanted to do.

I slumped in the back seat of the limo, happy that the day was over. I was mentally exhausted. My grandparents conceded on an American funeral in the States and would celebrate my mother for seven days straight once they got back to Ghana. Although it was their tradition, I couldn't survive a weeklong funeral because one day was hard enough.

It felt weird walking through my front door. The energy was different, and it smelled just like my mom. My grandparents settled into their guest suite while I laid in my mother's bed and cried with Ms. Alba.

A gentle knock rattled my mother's bedroom door.

"Come in," I said weakly.

My dad and my stepmother entered the room.

"Hey, sweetheart. I wanted to come see you before I headed back to my hotel for the night. It's been a long day for you, kiddo."

"Why can't you stay here with me? Do you have to stay in a hotel?" It was the least he could do since I barely knew him. Something inside of me was curious to learn more about him.

My step monster tensed up. She annoyed me and why the hell was she still wearing shades? We were inside the house.

"Yes, Mr. Santino, you can stay here. There is space and I can fix the other room up for you. I am sure that Nina would love to have you here with her."

"Excuse me, what is your name?" Nicole asked rudely.

"Alba. It's Alba, Mrs. Nicole."

"Where are you from? I can barely understand you." Taking off her shades, Nicole looked down at Ms. Alba.

"I am from El Salvador." Ms. Alba smiled nervously, wringing her hands.

"Well, Alba from El Salvador, it would be highly inappropriate for my husband to stay here tonight. We will go back to the Embassy Suites and come back in the morning." She slid her shades back on her face and stared until Ms. Alba turned and sat back on the bed with me.

"Ah, Nicole. You go back, dear," my dad said.

"What?" Nicole snapped, swinging her head in my father's direction. He was standing against the wall with his hands in his pocket.

"You're staying in THIS house tonight?" Nicole snatched her shades off and revealed raised brows, clutching the shades in the palm of her hand.

"I'm going to stay with Nina a little while longer. You can take the car. I'll uber back to the hotel. If Nina's needs me then I don't want to leave her."

She snatched up her purse, walked toward the door, and tripped over my shoes. I stifled a giggle by tucking my lips in.

"Alba? Is that your name?" Nicole spewed, looking back at Ms. Alba with narrowed eyes.

"Yes, Mrs. Nicole, that is my name."

"Can you straighten up a little better around here? I know today was a long day for everyone, however, it would've been bad if I would've fell over these shoes laying in the middle of the floor and hurt myself." Nicole sauntered out of the room then out of the house.

Once the wicked witch was gone, I turned to my dad and asked the question that everyone avoided.

"Dad, what will happen to me now? Can I live here with Ms. Alba or will I have to move to Africa with my uma and umpa?"

"Well, honey, I can tell you that you are not moving to Africa with your grandparents."

"Aden?" My umpa questioned as he walked into his late daughter's bedroom. He had his hands in his pockets, wearing a traditional African garment with a beautiful black and red tribal pattern.

My uma walked in behind him, quiet. She walked over to my mother's chaise lounge and picked up her throw blanket, bringing it to her nose to smell. She wrapped herself in the blanket and continued smelling it with a smile.

"With all due respect, sir, you and Mrs. Ayinde live on the other side of the world." My dad shifted his weight from one leg to another. "I'm her dad and I think Nina should be with me. I don't want her in Africa. It's way too far."

"Well, you were only a couple of states away and you never saw her anyway." The sheer panels fluttered as my umpa walked by them to stand near my uma. He rubbed her back and she sat quietly, clutching my mother's throw blanket.

"Whoa, that's not fair. I spoke to Nina occasionally and texted with her every so often. Please understand that I run a business and have a wife and three other kids." My dad's tone hardened a bit. I could tell he was offended.

"That's not my problem, Santino. You are full of excuses. You run a company and have three other kids. Nina is your first child, being a business owner does not mean you slack on being a father. I'm sure your new kids get the best of you while Nina and my daughter were left by the wayside." My umpa walked closer to my dad, looking up at him since he stood at only five foot ten.

"Excuse me? Are you saying that I lacked involvement with my daughter?"

"Yes. If you were involved, you were a quiet presence. So quiet that my daughter never mentioned you and your daughter hardly ever got to see you."

"I think you are overstepping now, sir. I know you are grieving. We all are. We all loved and will miss Ola." My dad was trying hard to give my umpa an excuse for his behavior.

"No Santino...*we* all love and miss Ola." My umpa pointed to me, my uma, and Ms. Alba when he stated *we*.

"You." My umpa was now jabbing my dad in the chest. "Don't love anyone but your high sa'ditty wife and your new kids." My dad looked at the floor then directly into my umpa's eyes. He was quiet, restraining himself from responding.

"Our granddaughter will come back to her home country where her mother was born and learn about the history of her roots. We are more than capable of taking care of her and we will provide her with everything she needs"

"Well, that's not happening and since I am her father, I trump you as a grandfather. Nina will live with me, and I will place her in private school with her siblings. She will get to know her siblings where she will live a life that she deserves." My dad stood firm and didn't move.

"So, she doesn't deserve to live with us because we are African?" My uma was now standing beside my umpa.

"I am not saying that. I am saying that she deserves to live with a parent."

"Umpa, Dad," I called out to them.

"Yes, honey. What did you want to say?" my dad asked.

"I don't want to move to Africa."

"I figured that, honey. It's okay. You will not move to another country." My dad pulled me closer and kissed the top of my head. I watched my grandparents closely. I was scared I hurt their feelings. My umpa shoulders slumped, and he sat near my uma who had returned to the chaise lounge. My uma was frozen and continued looking like she was in a daze. She wasn't focused on anything in particular.

"Dad. I don't want to move to North Carolina and live with you neither." I looked up at him with pleading eyes.

"Humph!" my umpa scoffed.

"Well, now I am baffled, baby. Where do you want to live?" my dad asked me.

"I want to live here with Ms. Alba. I want to stay in my own house with my mom's things." I sighed and sat on the bed near me. My dad rubbed the side of my face.

"I am not sure if that can happen, honey. I am sure Ms. Alba has a family of her own."

"She's mi familia," Ms. Alba said quietly.

"I understand that," my dad said sympathetically. "And believe me this is traumatic enough. I don't want to cause more trauma to Nina but who will maintain this house? Pay the bills? The taxes? It's a lot of moving pieces. Nina is still a minor which means I have to do what I think is the best possible option for her." My dad looked around at everyone in the room like he was on trial pleading his case.

"Daddy, I am closer to Ms. Alba than I am to anyone else in this room. I love all of you, but I have spent the last ten years of my life with my mom and Ms. Alba."

"I understand, honey, but who will pay Ms. Alba's salary now? What about her health insurance? It is so many grown up things that you do not understand." My dad was holding my chin with his hands. My tears came fast. I was at a loss for words. "Baby, let's not think about this right this second. Let's just try to get through the next couple of days."

"Sure." I wiped my nose with the back of my hand. I felt hopeless.

"Baby, I am going to go back to the hotel now and I will see you first thing in the morning, okay?"

"Sure, Dad." I was happy to see him leave. Ms. Alba got up and smoothed her dress.

"I will walk you out, Mr. Santino."

"Thanks Alba."

Chapter Seven

"Nina, you will be fine okay," Ms. Alba spoke softly.

I picked at my bacon, egg, and cheese bagel that she made for me. My stomach was in knots and I couldn't eat. I dreaded this day, but it was time to get back into a routine.

"Thank you," I said softly. "I miss her so much and I am so sad at the fight we had before she left."

"There was no fight, mi amor."

"Yes, there was, remember? She told me to clean my room because I was being a brat."

"That was a love dispute, not a fight."

I looked at Ms. Alba's perplexed while she kept two hands on the wheel and her eyes on the road. I didn't know if it was a cultural barrier or what, but she saw things differently.

"We are here, mi amor," she said, pulling up slowly to the drop off zone.

I eased out of my seat and opened the door slowly.

"Princess," Ms. Alba said, grabbing my arm gently.

"Yes ma'am?"

"I will be right here at the end of the school day waiting on you to pick you up, okay?"

"Yes, ma'am."

I walked into Bernard Academy and was met with tons of warm hugs and hellos.

It had been two weeks but now I was back in school. My dad flew back home, and my grandparents went back to Africa. My family agreed for me to stay in my house to finish out the school year under Ms. Alba's care, but I had no idea what life looked like for me after this. I flopped down in my seat. I didn't want to be at school.

"Nina, this is for you. Take your time and complete it and let me know if you have any questions on any of the materials," my teacher spoke in a delicate manner.

When I looked at the large manila envelope, I knew it was a ton of make-up assignments. I sighed heavily because I knew that I would get more of these packets as the day went on.

At lunch, one of my teammates spotted me and waved me to where she was sitting. I walked toward the table, sat down slowly, and opened my lunch box. There was chitter chatter all around me, but I drowned everyone out to sit in my thoughts.

"What do you think about that, Nina?"

"I'm sorry, what?" I responded not paying attention.

"That new girl Tamia. She has already made herself a reputation. We had a college fair, and her brother came in and spoke on behalf of his school and all the girls swooned over him. Now she's popular because everyone wants a chance to get close to her brother."

"Great," I said, not wanting to talk about her. I was too busy picking up the shattered pieces of my life. I didn't care about the new girl, or anything else at this point.

"Speaking of the new girl...heads up. She is walking this way with her entourage now."

It wasn't a heads up for me because I didn't care. I was secretly jealous of all of them because their mothers were still living. I looked at the toasted pastrami and cheese Ms. Alba made for me, unwrapping the aluminum foil.

"What's good, Nina?" Tamia asked, looking down at me.

Everyone sat around, staring at me like they were waiting for something eventful to happen. I realized at my mother's repass that everyone was laughing and eating moving on with their lives while mine stood still. Things were not normal for me anymore. I had no words and nothing for anyone. I ignored Tamia and everyone else around me and continued to nibble on my food.

"I'm sorry about your mom. What happened to her was so awful."

I perked up. I prayed that Tamia would leave. I felt like bursting into tears while blood rushed to my head.

"Are you going to say anything, Nina?" Tamia pressed on, smirking.

I placed my sandwich back into my lunch box and closed my water bottle. I wanted to bash Tamia's skull with my metal water bottle until she stopped talking.

I slammed the bottle on the table, causing everyone to jump. Standing up, I pushed past Tamia and her flunkies and walked toward my coach's room. I decided to eat my lunch alone, which was where I should have gone in the first place. Coach wasn't in her office, so I skipped school and went to a waterfall nearby.

"Hey, buddy," I spoke to the pigeons. I broke off a piece of bread from my sandwich and threw it on the ground. I smiled, watching the pigeon gobble up the bread.

I pulled out my notebook and started writing when I saw a shadow standing over me.

"Excuse me, young lady. Why aren't you in school?"

"Huh? The school I go to is out today. It's a teacher workday."

"Oh, really because I am the school resource officer at Bernard Academy, and I saw you leave out the side door and walk over here."

"Sir, it's my lunch period and I have permission to eat off site."

"Okay, that's good to know. Can I see your pass?"

"I'm sorry, what?"

"Can I see your pass? The one that you are assigned the beginning of the school year when you are granted permission to go off site for lunch. That is normally reserved for 11th and 12th graders, and I thought you were a 10th grader?"

"I think you have me confused with someone else, sir." I dismissed him and gathered my things. It's not like I had a mother he could call.

"Oh really? Because I thought you played volleyball for Coach Simpson and was her star sophomore that everyone raves about."

"Shit!" I said under my breath. There were pros and cons to being a student athlete.

"Yeah, that's what I figured. Come with me, young lady. You are not allowed to leave school grounds without a permission slip. I will have to take you into the office."

"Sir, can't you just allow me to go back to class?"

"That will be up to the faculty. My job is to make sure all the students are safe. When you enter this school in the mornings, your parents expect you to be safe in our care until the end of the school day."

"Don't you have more important things to do then bother me while I eat lunch and feed the birds?"

"Come on here and let's see how much talking you do when we call your parents."

Ha! I guess he didn't get the memo. I had no parent.

Ms. Alba had to come up to the school for what they considered an incident report. They released me and we made our way home in silence. Ms. Alba always talked, hummed, or something but today she was quiet.

"Ms. Alba, I wasn't gone for very long. They completely overreacted."

"Princess Nina, you should not have left school. They called your dad first. Then Santino called me in a panic. I had to leave work to come get you."

"You work?" My eyes bulged.

"Yes. I clean houses during your time at school for extra money."

"Is my dad not paying you?"

"I did this when your mom was alive too."

"I didn't know that, Ms. Alba." I thought Ms. Alba's only job was to care for me all these years. I had no idea she had a side hustle. It was weird how much I didn't know about her.

My phone buzzed and the familiar ringtone made me nervous.

Pressing the green button, I was cautious with my tone.

"Hello."

"Nina, what's going on. Why did you skip school today? It's your first day back for goodness sake!"

My dad was going on and on. I looked at Ms. Alba sideways. I couldn't believe that this man was yelling at me.

"Dad, I didn't feel like being in school because a girl said something smart to me about Mom at lunch today."

"Honey, I'm sorry. What did she say?" My dad's tone softened a bit.

"Nina, I heard about your mom and that's really awful." I squinted my eyes and shook my head when I repeated Tamia's words.

"Nina, what else did the child say?"

"That was it, Dad…. but it was not what she said, it was how she said it."

"How did she say it, Nina?"

"I think she was trying to be funny, Daddy."

"Are you sure? You don't think she was trying to be nice by welcoming you back and saying your mother's death was awful, which it was? If that's all that was said, then I don't see how that caused you to get so upset you left school. Not to mention you walked alone where you could have been abducted or hurt."

"Daddy, no one is stealing black girls that's close to six feet tall and all kids in the city walk alone." I rolled my eyes and dug my tongue into the top of my mouth.

"That's a lie. Traffickers are stealing all types of females young and old now a days. Nina, please do not make me regret my decision to leave you there with Alba to finish out the school year. Alba assured me she could handle this responsibility and you assured me that you would be fine."

"Daddy, I am fine! I just needed a moment!" I said, yelling at him. I was shocked at how he was coming at me when I hadn't seen him in ages before my mother's death.

Ranting and yelling, my dad went on and on. I took the phone from my ear and disconnected the call.

"I cannot believe you called him, Ms. Alba. I barely know him. You definitely don't know him, and you called him after I got into one small incident."

"Nina!" Ms. Alba said in the firmest voice that I had ever heard her use in my life.

"La escuela called him but if they hadn't, I would've had to call him anyway. It is part of our agreement. Do you know I had to beg Mr. Santino to let you stay with me and finish out the year? The only way he would agree is if I called and gave him updates on everything. If I do not keep him in the loop, then that means problemas for us because he will come and pick you up. Is that what you want? Es eso lo que quieres, Nina?"

My eyes were wide as saucers and I couldn't speak. For the first time in my life, Ms. Alba was yelling at me.

I was scared to answer so I said nothing.

"Respondeme!"

"No, ma'am," I answered swiftly. "That is not what I want."

"Then please no more skipping school."

Ms. Alba's phone rang when we pulled into the driveway.

"Hello, Mr. Santino," I heard her say. "No, no, she didn't hang up on you. Her cellphone died. I will have her call you back as soon as she charges it. We are walking into the house now."

Looking at me, she rolled her eyes, walked to her bedroom, and shut the door. Her bedroom was downstairs. I didn't want to push my luck, so I ran upstairs to my bedroom.

Chapter Eight

I decided to give school a try the next day. I didn't want to disappoint Ms. Alba. I promised her I would do my best to have a great day. She smoothed things over with my dad and I didn't want to mess that up neither. Most importantly, I didn't want to let my mother down.

The truth of the matter was that I felt like an outsider. I no longer belonged to anyone who loved me unconditionally. My security was gone. Tamia found me at a weak moment and decided to take advantage of it. I heard she had spread rumors of running me off. What Tamia didn't understand was that she was now in danger. The rage I felt with the world was bottled up inside of me and everyday it took every ounce of energy that I could muster to keep it contained. I wanted someone to feel the emptiness that I felt and while Tamia had a home with two parents, I didn't have one procreator waiting for me when I walked through the threshold of my house. Ms. Alba was there but it wasn't the same.

I couldn't sleep because I dreamt about my mother's funeral. I couldn't eat because my stomach was always in knots, and I couldn't feel because I was numb from sadness. I was going to find Tamia. She was becoming a thorn in my side and as much as I tried to ignore her, she kept popping up. I wanted to get to the bottom of what was going on once and for all. I prayed that God granted me mercy and grace for the disturbance embedded in my soul.

I watched the clock on the wall. I hadn't heard anything the teacher said. I wanted it to be over so I could find Tamia during lunch and handle her. When the bell finally rang, I bolted out of my seat, grabbed my books, and made a beeline toward the door.

I walked straight over to Tamia and busted up the conversation with her friends. "Tamia, can I speak with you for a moment?" I had my hand on my hip and my weight rested on one leg.

"Nah, I'm busy." She turned her head and continued talking as if I was not there. I moved closer to her. I felt my insides heating up. I closed my eyes and tried to remember my promise to Alba and my dad.

I tapped her shoulder harder.

"Tamia, I'm going to ask you again. Can I talk to you for a minute?"

Tamia turned around and stood in my face.

"We have nothing to talk about. Everybody knows when I tried to talk to you last time you ran off!"

"I didn't run off. I walked off it was because your breath was so stank, I couldn't bear it." I was so close to Tamia's face that our noses almost touched.

"Oooohhh!" Tamia's friends laughed at my comment. One boy had his fist over his mouth and jumped up and down.

Tamia pushed me so hard that I stumbled. My nostrils flared and I exploded. I jumped up and grabbed Tamia by her hair. I mushed her face into the cafeteria tray. Her arms flailed as she tried to reach back and remove my grip, but my strength was no match for her. I knew she would be able to go home and cry to her mother, but I couldn't. My mother was gone, and I was angry. Those thoughts made me mush her face harder. When I let her go, mashed potatoes and corn filled her face. Everyone laughed except Tamia. She cried.

 I glared at her as I backed away slowly.

"Hopefully, this clears up our little misunderstanding. Now leave me the hell alone and don't let my name come out of your mouth again."

I grabbed my backpack and made my way to my coach's room. I had butterflies in my stomach while I sat and ate my lunch alone. I waited patiently for faculty to escort me out to call Ms. Alba to get me. However, that never happened. I went on with the rest the school day. I even went to practice and had a great run.

Two hours later, I was making my way out the school, waiting for Ms. Alba to pick me up.

"Hey, Ms. Alba," I said as I got into her car.

"Hey, mi amor. How was school today?" I wasn't sure if this was a trick question. I looked out the corner of my eye.

"Fine, how was your day? Did you clean any houses today?"

"Yes. I cleaned one house today. It was small and only took a few hours. I have something special planned for us when we get home today."

The butterflies in my stomach came back. I prayed that the something special didn't include my dad being in the living room, ready to take me to his home. Ms. Alba didn't mention anything about getting a call from the school, but I was waiting for it to blow up in my face.

We entered the house through the garage and the smell of spices filled the air. I showered quickly and went downstairs to a crockpot of chili. I loved when Ms. Alba had dinner waiting because I was always starving after practice.

"Do you have any homework, Nina?" Ms. Alba asked.

"I sat in the coach's classroom and completed my work during lunch."

"Good, that means that we can get to my surprise. Let's go in the bonus room."

I walked to the bonus room. I wondered if my dad would be in there.

"Surprise, Princess Nina." Ms. Alba had her hands in the air and smiled.

My eyes surveyed the floor. There were tons of photos, pictures albums, glue, decorative stickers, and card stock materials.

"I thought it would be a great idea for us to create some scrapbooks with all the memories and good times we had with your mama."

"Wow, Ms. Alba, where did you get some of these photos from?" My eyes misted as I sat on my knees and looked through vacation pictures, holiday pictures, and my baby pictures with my mom.

"I got them from your mother's picture boxes and some of them were photos that I captured over the years."

I had never seen some of these images before. There were even photos of my parents together when they were young.

The doorbell rang.

"I have one more surprise for you, mi amor." Ms. Alba jumped up and grabbed a cloth.

"Who's at the door?"

"You will see but let me put this blindfold on you."

"Blindfold? Why?"

"Because I want you to be surprised, Nina. Now, stay here and don't move."

"Okay." I bit my bottom lip while I waited.

After what seemed like forever, Ms. Alba came back. I heard whimpering, then I felt something lick my face. I smiled from ear to ear and snatched off my blindfold. I hollered.

"A dog, Ms. Alba! You got me a dog!"

"Yes. I feel like he will do you some good. Whenever you feel sad or lonely because you are missing your mom, you can talk to him. He's a good listener and he will never talk back or interrupt you."

We burst into laughter. It was a brown, ten-pound Shicon.

"What are you going to name him?"

"Teddy. I want to name him Teddy."

Chapter Nine

My home life was great with Teddy. Ms. Alba had purchased some dog clothes, but Teddy wasn't the type of dog that kept on clothes.

"Ms. Alba, can we make brownies tonight?"

"Sure thing, Princess Nina."

Teddy started barking.

"What's up, Teddy? You want brownies too, buddy?"

"No brownies for the perro...chocalate is a no for dogs."

"Oh, I didn't know that Ms. Alba."

BOOM

Our front door exploded and slammed against the wall.

"Hands up! Nobody move!" one man, in a vest all-black, screamed.

"What's going on?" I jumped and yelled hysterically.

"Who are you!"

"What are you doing in our home?"

"Alba Mendez?" a bald short man questioned, looking at Ms. Alba.

Ms. Alba was frozen. Her color left her skin, and her eyes were vacant.

"Ms. Alba, what do they want? How do they know you?"

"Young lady, we are I.C.E. We got tipped off that Alba is staying here as an illegal immigrant. We have to send her back to her country. She is being deported."

"What does that mean? Ms. Alba, what does that mean? Tell them that you live here with me. Tell them it's not true."

Ms. Alba didn't say a word. She looked at me with shame and sorrow in her eyes. I screamed and kicked the officers restraining me.

"Te Quiero, Princesa Nina," she whispered. Ms. Alba placed her head down before they escorted her out the door.

"Let me go! Let me go!" I broke away from the officers and ran up to Ms. Alba, hugging her neck.

"Please, don't leave me. Please, don't forget me. I love you, Ms. Alba."

"Lo siento," she whispered, unable to hug me back.

Chapter Ten

"I like those earrings."

When I looked up, I saw a heavyset girl, wearing a dingy, white sweatshirt that barely covered her belly. I tried to read her face, noticing her short hair that struggled to meet the hair clip sitting on top of her head. The girl had been eyeing me since I got into the group home. I ignored her and I sat on my cot, looking around. All eyes were on me, and I was scared shitless.

"I said I like those earrings. Are they real?" She touched my ears and I flinched, swatting her hand away.

"Get off me! Don't touch me."

"I was just trying to be nice, bitch!" She pushed me and my head made a loud thud against the wall.

"Ouch!" I was in a daze. I wasn't sure if I should try to fight this linebacker or look like a punk, so I sat back against the wall. I looked around at the other four girls. They stared at me with poker faces. I didn't know whether they were friends with the linebacker or not. I focused hard on not crying when one girl finally spoke.

"Don't worry, girl. She's like that with everybody." The tall, skinny girl had bad acne. Her teeth were jumbled up and yellow.

"How long have you been here?" I asked.

"Too long. Where you parents at?"

"My mom died, and my dad is out of state."

"Where are your parents?"

"They are both crackheads. I ain't seen them since I was little."

"Oh," was all that I could say.

"All right, ladies! Lights out!" The harsh voice came from a chiseled faced woman with stiff shoulders. She canvased the area with squinted eyes and flipped the lights. I didn't move. I stayed sitting with my knees pulled to my chest and my back against the cold, hard wall.

"Hey, new girl. What's your name?"

"Nina."

"Are you going to lay down or are you going to sit up all night?"

"I'm not tired."

"Shut the fuck up! I am trying to get my rest," the linebacker yelled from across the room.

I sighed. I was scared. I felt like this was going to be hell. My heart was heavy at the thought of this being my new life. How could my life change so drastically within a day?

"Hey, Mona!" the skinny girl next to me yelled across the room.

"What?" the linebacker snapped. *So, her name is Mona,* I thought to myself.

"New girl said you shut the fuck up!"

"No, I didn't!" I screamed at her. My eyes were as wide as saucers.

"Yes, you did! I heard you!"

Before I could approach this skinny, less intimidating bitch, the linebacker snatched my long, thick ponytail and plunged me onto the concrete floor. I clasped my hands around her closed fist. I tried to remove her grip from my hair.

Whap

She punched me in my face. Blows were coming from everywhere and I realized that unless the linebacker was an octopus with eight arms, someone else was helping her.

"Ahhh! Help! Help!" I screamed to the top of my lungs. I tried blocking my face then I felt a kick in my back. I fell to the floor. I felt a barefoot kick the side of my face. I tasted blood on the inside of my jaw.

"Get off me! Get off me!" I swung wildly, but the blows

kept coming from everywhere.

"Stop! Help!" I yelled.

Someone took off my sneaker. My ears burned. I felt flesh rip when someone snatched out my earrings. My t-shirt and my bra were ripped off then I felt sharp teeth bite my nipple. I cried while punching whomever it was in the head repeatedly. Bright lights came on and all the girls scrambled like roaches.

"Break it up in here! All right!! All right, break it up in here!"

I wailed like a baby in the middle of the floor, bloodied and half-naked. I held my hand up to my ears. My head was pounding like it was going to explode.

"Who's responsible for this?" the female staff worker asked.

No one spoke.

"What is your name?"

"Nina," I said barely audible.

"Are you okay?"

"No." I cried.

"Call the social worker," I heard someone say in the background.

"Nina, let's get you up. Gather your things."

The worker helped me stand up, but my leg buckled, and I fell back down. My ankle felt like it was broke, my breast was exposed, and I tried to cover up.

"Where is your overnight bag? Let's get you a shirt," the

worker said.

"Over there." I pointed toward the bed, but it was gone.

"Where is my bag!" I demanded, my voice hoarse. I cried and looked around. The girls didn't move.

"Someone took my bag!"

"Alright who has her things? I am only going to ask once."

"The bag is right there," one of the girls said. My bag was across the room, but it was empty.

"Where is all my stuff?" I yelled. I crawled on my hands and knees and snatched my bag. My clothes, cellphone, and toiletries were all gone.

"Who took my stuff?" I screamed at the top of my lungs. I was shaking and walking around the room, looking for my things.

"Ma'am, they stole my stuff. Where is my mother's picture?" I yelled. I didn't care about the other things as much as I cared about the one picture that I grabbed of me and my mom with Ms. Alba before leaving my home. I.C.E didn't give me much time to pack a bag, but I managed to grab that photo and now it was gone.

"Alright, girls. I am going to take her to get her cleaned up and when I get back all of her things better be returned or everyone in here will be facing some harsh consequences."

I grabbed my blanket off my cot the and the worker covered me up, helping me out of the room.

"Ah!" I yelped in pain. My ankle was tender and swollen. The worker helped clean me up and wrapped my ankle. I was sitting in the lobby, elevating my foot on another chair when the front door burst open. The noise jarred me.

"Daddy!" I yelled. I dropped the blanket and limped toward him.

"Nina? Nina, baby, what happened? Oh my God, baby. What happened to you? Who did this to you? What happened to my fucking daughter!" my dad yelled.

The staff didn't have answers other than saying things like this sometimes happens. I sobbed like a baby. I had never been happier to see a familiar face in my life. The last 24 hours had been as horrific as finding out that my mom was killed.

It felt weird walking into my home. I looked around searching for my puppy frantically.

"Daddy, where's Teddy?" I asked.

"Who's Teddy, baby?"

"He's my dog. Ms. Alba bought him for me."

"I don't know, baby. They probably called animal control to come get him," he said carefully, being delicate with his words.

I let my emotions flood through my eyes like a levee broke and cried.

"Nina, it's okay, baby. You have had a rough couple of months. I know it's a lot to handle for a fourteen-year-old."

"Why is all of this happening to me?"

"I don't know, baby, but we will get through it. I am here now, and I wish I would've taken you home with me right after your mother's funeral." When he hugged me, I inhaled a spicy, sandalwood fragrance that was a welcome change from the group home's stale odor.

"Look at me. I am so sorry this happened to you. I'm sorry that I haven't been more of a presence in your life. I'm also sorry that we lost your mom. She was my first true love."

My dad had tears in his eyes, but they didn't fall.

"Let's get you cleaned up. I will run you a bath and we need to pack up a few things because our flight leaves in the morning to go home."

"What about my mommy's home? What about all of my stuff here and my mom's things? What will happen to it?" My questions came out quickly. "What about my school? I have a big game coming up."

My dad sat on the edge of the sofa and patted the spot next to him. He turned to me, held my hands, and looked into my eyes.

"Nina, I'm going to be really honest with you. I don't have answers to all your questions. We will have to take it one day at a time. Right now, I will have to contact your grandparents and possibly hire an estate attorney to figure things out. We can place your mother's items in storage, that way you will always have them."

I took a deep breath. My dad made me feel like he was about to say something that I didn't want to hear.

"You will definitely be changing schools. Don't worry because you will make new friends and you have siblings that will be in the same school with you to help you transition into your new life."

"Daddy, I don't want a new life. I want my old life back."

"I know, honey, but unfortunately that's not possible."

"What about Ms. Alba? What will happen to her?"

"I don't know," my dad whispered, squeezing my hands.

I went to my room and walked into my bathroom.

"Arghhhh!" My reflection in the mirror was unrecognizable. I hadn't seen myself until now.

"What's wrong?" My dad ran into my room, panting and holding his chest.

"Look at what those girls did to my face, Daddy!"

"I know, baby. It will heal and the swelling will go down."

"Oh my God! Look at my hair! They cut my ponytail! Why would they do that to me?"

"Your hair will grow back, baby, and we will go to the dentist as soon as we get to North Carolina."

"What? The dentist?" I turned around and pressed my top and bottom teeth together to look at my teeth. My front tooth was chipped. My lip was busted and my eye was bruised. My ankle was swollen, and my left breast was throbbing.

I cried while taking a bath. I felt numb. I wanted to slide under the bubbles until the water choked the air from my lungs.

"Are you okay in there?"

"Yes." I jumped up in the tub. "I'm okay," I said weakly.

I dragged myself from the tub, dried off, and put on my pajamas. My dad walked in and sat at the foot of the bed. He tucked me in, kissed my forehead, and told me get a good night's sleep. It proved to be impossible with my head pounding from the beating I received. I got up after tossing and turning for thirty minutes to get a bottle of water and painkillers to ease my headache. I heard my dad crying as I walked back upstairs. I pressed my ear to the wall and peeked over the banister into the living room downstairs. My dad kissed my mom's photo and placed it back down on the bookshelf.

Delia Rouse

Chapter Eleven

M y stomach was in knots as we rode in my dad's car service to my new home. My head was turned toward my window as I took in all the plush greenery and massive plots of empty land. The air smelled like freshly cut grass. Raleigh, North Carolina was a far cry from the city.

"We're here," my dad said. He smiled and waved his arm, proud of his home.

The car stopped in front of a massive estate. The driver opened the door and helped me out of the car.

"Come on, baby. The whole family is inside and can't wait to meet you!"

My dad led me up the brick stairs. The door swung open before he touched the knob.

"Hello, Nina. Do you remember me? I'm your Grandma Sabrina, and this is your Grandpa Richard." They hugged me at the same time. "This is your Great Grandma Diane and your Great Grandpa Mario. They are your Grandpa Richard's parents"

"Wow," I said in awe. "You have grown up young lady. I think you were about two or three the last time we saw you." She touched the side of my face with her wrinkled hand that held a stunning diamond ring placed on her French manicured finger. I was uncomfortable. I still had some swelling from my fight. "Wow, she has deep dimples just like our Santino."

"You are a stunning young lady." My great grandpa smiled, leaning his upper body back slightly with his hands in his pockets.

"Thank you," I said quietly.

"Nina," my dad said softly, placing his hands on my shoulders. I winced in pain.

"These are your siblings. This is your little brother, Greyson. This is your younger sister, Riley, and your sister Ryan."

"Hello." I smiled weakly. They hugged me one by one.

"Hello, honey." My stepmother smiled.

"Hello, Nicole," I said without emotion.

"You can call me mom," she said.

No, the fuck I will not!

"Honey, I know you had a rough couple of days. We have your room all made up for you and Maria, our family helper, will take your bags to your new room and show you your new space. Welcome home, honey." My stepmother hugged me like she really cared. I wasn't sure how to feel about her just yet. The hug felt forced and insincere.

"That can wait until later, Nicole." My Grandma Sabrina shut Nicole down quickly, holding her hand up. "Let the family get to know her and welcome her properly. We don't want to shun her to her room, she just got here. Come on, honey, let's go into the dining room and get you something to eat. Are you hungry?"

"Yes, ma'am, a little bit." She grabbed my waist and led me into the massive dining room.

I surveyed my new family while at the table. They were a beautiful set of people, but I couldn't help but notice that they looked nothing like me. All of them except for my granddad and his parents looked like they were mixed or creole. I was the only sepia tone person in the room, and it felt awkward. I was used to my mother's African ancestral looking people.

"Nina, I like your afro," my new younger sister Ryan said.

"Thanks, while I was in the group home the girls jumped me and cut all my hair off." I was used to having long, thick hair. I felt embarrassed. I looked down at my feet then picked my nails.

"What!" my grandfather yelled. "Santino, you didn't tell us that!"

"Yeah, she got into a tussle with some of the other girls."

"Actually," I said, cutting my dad off. "They jumped me, stole all my clothes, cut my hair, and ripped my earrings out of my ears. They also caused me to chip my front tooth." My face tingled at the way he tried to downplay my experience.

Everyone gathered around me, looking at my war wounds and asking me a ton of questions. Nicole was sitting at the far end of the table with her elbows resting in front of her and her hands clasped together. She was uninterested in my trauma at the group home.

"Nina, don't worry," Ryan said. "We have a personal hair stylist, and she can give you some dope braids. Her name is Nakema, and she's sick with her skills."

"Really?"

"Yes. Hold up, let me text her real quick. Dad, if she has a slot open can we go now and get Nina hooked up before we take her to start school? You know she gotta be straight when she walks up into The Higher Learning Academy." Ryan was texting fast.

My dad looked happy. His shoulders bounced up and down.

"Sure, honey, hook her up." My dad put his hands in the air while doing air quotes.

"Nina, while we are waiting for her to text us back, let me show you to your room." Riley scooted her chair back from the table to stand up. "My mom wanted to get our interior decorator to fix the room up for you, but I told her to let it stay neutral so that you can put your own spin on it since it is your room." Riley was going a mile a minute and I loved every bit of it. I was my mother's only child so having sisters seemed like it was going to be a lot of fun.

"I also just got a new Beamer for my sweet sixteenth

birthday, so we don't' have to have Daddy's car service or Maria drive us around like a bunch of squares. You can drive my car until you get…"

"No!" Nicole yelled abruptly, cutting Riley off.

Everyone snapped their heads around and looked at Nicole, who was slightly red. It wasn't hard for her to accomplish since she was pale with pink undertones.

"I mean, we don't want to break the law because Nina obviously does not have a North Carolina license or permit yet being that she just moved here, and we don't have her on our insurance." Nicole was blinking rapidly, looking from person to person at the table.

"No biggie," my grandma said, lifting her hand in the air again. It was clear she reigned supreme in this family. "Nina, baby, do you have a permit yet?"

"No, ma'am," I responded.

"Are you interested in learning how to drive?"

"Yes, ma'am." I was excited for the first time since I got here.

"It is settled then. We'll get you personal driving lessons," Grandma Sabrina declared.

"They give lessons in school, Mother Sabrina. Remember, that is how Riley learned," Nicole stated.

"We are not talking about Riley, Nicole. We're talking about Nina. My granddaughter has been through enough trauma, and I don't want her taking mass lessons with a bunch of ghetto unruly kids. I think personalized private lessons will be a better fit for her and so that's what she will get." The look in my grandmother's eyes let Nicole know that her words were final, and the discussion was over.

"Maria!" Grandma Sabrina yelled. "Get a pen, honey, and write this down for me so that I won't forget." Maria scurried to the butler's pantry to get a pen and pad.

"Set up driving lessons for Nina."

"Set up a jewelry showing so that she can get new earrings. Hmmm, what else, son?" my grandmother asked my dad, tapping the tips of her fingers on the dining room table.

"We need to get her a new phone. Those heathen children stole hers," my dad said angrily.

"Make her an emergency dental appointment," my great grandmother said, pointing toward Maria to write it down.

"Set up a couple of therapy sessions," my Grandpa Richard chimed in. "Let her talk through some of what she has been through with a professional. That's if you're comfortable with that, sweetheart?" He looked over at me.

"Yes, I can try it," I said, hunching my shoulders. At that moment, I remembered my mom saying to me to never be ashamed to talk about my problems.

I looked around the dining room table at everyone talking and making plans for my transition into the family. It felt nice that I was getting so much love and attention from my new family. It also felt a little weird because they were all still strangers to me, including my dad. When I looked over at Riley, she crossed her eyes and stuck her tongue out to the side. She placed her pointer finger to her head and moved it around in circles. We burst out laughing. I noticed that my stepmother was gone, but I hadn't noticed when she left.

"Let's bounce," Riley whispered to me. "Let me take you to see the rest of our house."

We slipped away while everyone barked orders to Maria. Riley took me through the kitchen and up back stairs that went straight into a massive bonus room.

"This is where we hang out."

"Whoa, this is a nice movie room."

"Yeah, it's cool. Come on, let me show you your room."

Riley pointed out everyone's rooms as we walked down the hallway.

"Our parents' room is through the double doors at the end of the hall." My room was on the complete opposite end of the hall.

"This is your room."

I walked into my room in awe. It was beautiful. It had a queen size canopy bed with a trundle. A candle flickered on a large wooden shelf that smelled like vanilla bean. The plush comforter had decorative pillows and looked like something from a catalogue. I walked toward a grey love seat with a high back in a small sitting area and ran my hands across the tufted, diamond shaped buttons. I looked out the double paned window and the plush green lawn had diagonal lines as if it was freshly cut.

Riley's cell phone chimed.

"Hey, this is my boyfriend texting me let me call him real quick while you finish checking out your room. The bathroom and closet are through that door over there. I'll be right back."

"Sure," I said, smiling. I loved my room. It wasn't my normal taste, but it was beautiful. I wanted to show Nicole my appreciation and tell her thank you since she set this up for me. I walked down the hall where Riley told me she and my dad slept. The walls were filled with art and wood carved accent walls.

One of the double doors was open so I slid in. The room was empty, so I walked around. The furnished seating area was beautiful with a full-blown living room set. Another set of double doors led to their bathroom. Walking through I could see Nicole's reflection in a full-length mirror that towered against the wall. She was standing at the island in the middle of her closet. I watched her for a moment to think of a way to tell her thank you and break the awkward tension between us. As I lifted my hand to gently rake my knuckles against the door, I saw Nicole lift a big vase and hurled it into the mirror.

I jumped back and darted out the room, nervous and scared. I decided it would be safer for me to join the rest of the family back in the dining room.

"Hey guys." Nicole sauntered in with a silver tray holding several glasses filled with lemonade. My body stiffened.

"I have an idea. I think we should throw Nina a welcome party. That way we can introduce her to the rest of the family and all of our friends."

"That's a great idea, honey." My dad said and the grands agreed.

"I want to show my oldest daughter off to everyone," my dad said.

"Our *daughter*, honey," Nicole, corrected him.

"You're right... our daughter."

"Then it's settled. One month from today. That will give me a little over four weeks to plan everything. Nina, me and you have a date to go shopping so that we can find you something stunning to wear for your party."

"Ok," I said, wringing my hands together. "Thank you so much for everything."

"No problem, sweetheart. Your family," she said with that fake plastered smile.

Delia Rouse

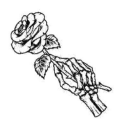

Chapter Twelve

T he Higher Learning Academy was a beautiful private school. My favorite part of the school was the waterfalls throughout the campus and the designated areas outside for students to eat lunch, congregate, or have class if the teacher decided to lecture outdoors. There were wrought iron tables and chairs painted in maroon and white and a big eagle in the grass spray painted with the school's mascot colors. My school back home was in the middle of the city and although the school was considered one of the best schools for the gifted in NY, it wasn't private, and the grounds weren't as impressive as my new school campus.

The school provided the students with personal MacBooks,

and lockers that were designed to hang our MacBooks from the front of them, which was strange to me because in New York we locked up our personal items.

My new school mimicked my old school with a majority white student body; however, the students were friendly. Riley and Ryan were popular and introduced me as their sister from New York, they also took me to meet some of the student athletes. I was interested in connecting with some of the volleyball players and planned on trying out for the team. My nerves were all over the place because I could tell by the expansive trophy cases along the school halls that they had a top tier athletic program. Volleyball was the only thing that still brought me joy and I decided to dedicate my anxious and melancholy energy to the sport that my mom enjoyed watching me play.

This morning, Nicole told me that she would pick me up and instructed Ryan and Riley to leave without me. My stomach did flips when the day ended, and I approached the car. Mr. Bernie, our driver, was standing outside of the car waiting on me with Nicole inside.

An awkward silence filled the car.

"Nina, I wanted us to spend some quality time together which is why I told my girls they couldn't come. Since you have been with us; we haven't had a chance to bond." Nicole was looking out the window. She had on oversized sunglasses with her legs crossed. Her perfectly manicured toes were on display in her strapped, three-inch heel sandals.

"Okay." I sat like a statue, not wanting to make a wrong move or say the wrong thing.

The car stopped in front of a boutique. I looked at Nicole and she didn't move. The driver opened her door for her to step out of the car. I farted when I exhaled because I was nervous. I opened my door quickly to catch up with Nicole but hit Bernie with the door.

"Oh no, I'm so sorry."

"Nina!"

"Yes, ma'am" I jumped, startled by her tone.

"We don't open doors. We have doors opened for us," Nicole snapped.

"Okay," I said, looking at Bernie and mouthed *sorry*. He rubbed his chin where the top of the door frame smacked him.

"Hello, Mrs. Wellington," several people greeted us. She must've shopped at the boutique on the regular.

"Hello, Morgan. Please pull some looks for my daughter. I want something formal, nice, and flowy. Give me a variety of options for a dinner party I will be hosting."

"Mrs. Wellington, this sounds fabulous," the associate squealed.

I looked around at the clothes in awe. My mom bought me beautiful clothes all the time but nothing this fancy and luxurious. I saw a tailor onsite, hemming a woman's dress in the back.

"Wow...it's like everything in here can be custom fitted." I was thinking out loud, not realizing that the words came out.

Nicole turned and looked at me perplexed.

"I know that you are used to big box clothing stores; however, there is no fit like a custom fit." I shook my head up and down, smiled, and walked toward a coral maxi dress trimmed in rhinestones. I extended my hands. The fabric was beautiful, and I wanted to try it on.

"Nicole, I think I may have found a dress!" Nicole looked around the store like she was embarrassed. She walked toward me briskly.

"You can call me mother, my dear."

"That's so kind of you but since my mom is dead and she's the one that raised me, I rather not use that term. Is there anything else I can call you instead of Nicole?" She walked toward the dress, ignoring my question.

"This is beautiful, dear."

"I think so too. Can I try it?" I was excited at the possibility of owning a gown so beautiful.

"I'm not sure that the color coral suits you. It may be a little too bright for your skin tone." She had her pointer finger against her top lip, bouncing it up and down.

My eyes bulged and I stood, frozen. I never had an adult comment on my complexion in a negative way before. School kids, yes. The media, yes. My mom always told me they were brainwashed assholes by society's standard of thinking that European beauty was the only beauty acceptable.

"Morgan! Morgan! Do you have this dress here in

black? My daughter is fond of it."

"Nicole." I was walking on eggshells, speaking in the smallest voice I could muster. "I don't like the color black or fresh flowers. It reminds me of my mother's funeral."

"Awe, dear, come here to momma." She placed her hands on both sides of my face. I held my breath and closed my eyes. I wasn't sure what was coming next, and I cringed at her referring to herself as *momma*.

"Do you think I'm pretty?"

"Huh?" I opened my eyes, frowning my brow lines. I looked at her as if I didn't understand her question.

"You heard me; do you think I'm pretty?"

"Yes. Yes, I-I-I think you're beautiful," I stuttered.

"Okay, then trust my choices, dear. Did your father tell you that I used to be a model back in my day?"

"No, he didn't tell me that."

"Yes, honey. I walked the runways with the best of them. I've maintained my size four all these years. So, please trust momma on this. Fashion is what I do, and I can look at you and already tell you what will work and what will not. That color on you will not work."

"Mrs. Wellington, we do not have that dress in black but here are four others that you can have your daughter try on."

"Thank you, Morgan, these are perfect."

"This one." Nicole pointed at a plain, long, black dress that lacked personality. It looked like it was for an old person not a teenager.

"Try this," she spoke knowingly, looking down and feeling the fabric while Morgan agreed with her dress choice.

"Nicole," I said weakly. She snapped her head up. She seemed irritated.

"Yes, daughter," she said, pronouncing the word loud and deliberately.

"Do you know when the movers will get to North Carolina with my stuff?"

"About that, honey." I perked up and walked closer to her.

"I got a rather upsetting call. There was an accident of some sort while the movers were packing up your home. Most things were salvaged but your mother's urn was destroyed."

"Nooooo!" I screamed.

"Yes, dear. I'm sorry but things happen sometimes that are out of our control."

I backed up and shook my head with tears streaming down my face. I ran out of the store and ran straight into my dad, who was stepping out of his four-door black on black Maserati.

"Nina! What's wrong? What is going on? I was coming to surprise you guys and take you to lunch." I was hyperventilating and telling him what Nicole had told me.

"What?" he asked, grabbing my shoulders.

He looked up and Nicole was walking out of the store toward us.

"Nicole, how in the hell did this happen? I told you to pay

for white glove service and to stipulate that the urn was to be crated and wrapped securely!"

"Honey, I did."

My dad took his phone out to make a call.

"Santino, honey, let me handle it. I will take care of it."

Nicole put her hands on my dad's shoulders. I buried my face deep into his broad chest and cried. I felt Nicole breasts on my back as she placed her arm around my neck, hugging me from behind. Nicole kissed the back of my head and looked at my dad with tears running down her face.

"Honey I will not sleep until I get to the bottom of what happened to Omalara' s urn. I have already decided to file a complaint and I will follow through as soon as we get home."

"Nina," my dad spoke, pulling us out of Nicole's embrace. "I didn't anticipate being met with such horrible news. I apologize for not carrying Mommy on the plane with us like you suggested. I will have Nicole see if they can salvage some ashes so that we can make you a locket. That way you can carry your mother around your neck and close to your heart every day and all day."

That small gesture made me feel a little better, but I was still distraught.

"That was all that I had left of her, Daddy." My speech was inaudible because I was sobbing.

"You have her memories and her blood runs through your heart. That can never be destroyed."

"Nicole," my dad said sharply, snapping her out of her

gaze.

"Yes, honey."

"Let me know the moment you hear what happened up there. I want specifics. I want names. I want heads to roll. And I want someone to take accountability."

"Yes, dear," Nicole responded solemnly.

Chapter Thirteen

"Nina, come downstairs quick. I have some good news I want to share with you."

"I'm right here, Dad." I was standing behind him, looking out the windows and wondering what all the fuss was about. Nicole was standing in the corner. She then walked toward us.

"The good news is the moving truck is here with your things from New York."

"Yay, when did they arrive, Daddy? I am so excited I can't wait to get some of my things and my mom's things in my possession I've been without them for way too long."

"I know, honey. I don't know what took this move so long and I'm really still upset about them breaking your mother's urn, but they are bringing in what they were able to salvage from the accident. Nicole, did you ever follow up with what happened?"

"Yes, honey, I did. Breaking the urn was simply human error. They gave us fifty percent off the cost of the move but unfortunately, Santino, there was nothing they could do to salvage any of the ashes," she whispered to my dad.

"That's heartbreaking, we can't change what has happened but what I would like for you to do, darling, is to make sure that you incorporate as much of Nina's items as possible into this new life she shares with us. This house is lavish but it's not her style. Her room is meticulously decorated, and I appreciate you trying but I would like for her to have the vibrant and bright colors that she had in her home that she shared with her mother. She has basically nothing left of her mom but memories. Since the urn is gone, do your best and make sure she's happy and as comfortable as possible in her new space."

"I have to go to work, ladies. I'll be back later tonight. Have fun, Nina, and let the movers know exactly where you want things and what we cannot fit we will put in the storage unit located in the very back of our property." He grabbed the top of my shoulders and kissed my forehead then pecked Nicole on the lips.

"Thank you, Daddy," I said, excited to be able to get some of my personal items incorporated into my room. I had a dire need to have items that connected me to my old life. This life was so different from what I was used to, and I felt so removed from my mother's memory.

One of my favorite things about my new bedroom was my big walk-in closet. It was L-shaped with a little hidden cubby. Nicole placed a vanity in the small-cubed space, but I removed it to hang my long dresses and coats in that space. One of my passions was drawing and I began creating a mural of my mother on the back wall, the dresses helped me cover it. I didn't think Nicole would approve of me drawing a picture of my mother on her walls, but even if she did, something inside of me wanted this piece of my mother's memory to myself. I needed to feel a connection to her that was sacred to me. Especially since her urn was destroyed during the move.

When I was little, my mother taught me how to draw. It was one of my favorite things to do with her because she was a fabulous artist. I always started with the eyes, I wanted them to be perfect and catch the essence of my mother's eyes.

Something deep inside me told me that Nicole would be furious. She seemed very possessive of my father, and I was not only drawing on the wall, but I was drawing a picture of a woman who reminded her that my dad had a love before he married her. Thankfully, she never spent time or dealt with me so I never expected her to enter my room but having a way to hide my picture would make me feel better just in case she wandered into my private space.

"Nina," Nicole said sharply, snapping me out of my trance. I was staring out of the window at the movers.

"I know you're excited about receiving your things and the movers are working swiftly to get as much as your stuff upstairs as possible, but the majority will be in the storage facility on the back of the estate. I also want to remind you that this huge welcoming party that I meticulously planned for you is tonight it starts at seven sharp and because this party is for you, darling, I need you to make sure that you're ready and on time. We don't do late around here."

"Okay, I'll be ready."

Nicole looked at me with a frown.

"Why did you take your braids out?"

"My head was itching, and it was time for a really good wash. I had them in for three weeks and it was time for them to come out. My mom always told me if I braided my hair, never leave them in too long because it would create matting and tangles, causing breakage."

"Well, with the little bit of hair you have I would think it would've been more presentable if you would've gotten your hair re-braided in time for my fabulous party."

I let out a small gasp. I wasn't sure how I felt about the way she said the word *presentable*. It hurt my feelings, and I wanted to make sure I understood her clearly. For some reason, I didn't want to disappoint her.

"Nicole, my hair will be presentable it will just be in its natural state. I've washed, conditioned, and oiled it. Once I unravel the twist, it will be a beautiful short twist out." I smiled. I took my right hand and extended my twist. I was excited about my new look.

"Right...right, honey. The thing is your hair is a different texture from what I'm used to so I'm not sure if your version of a twist out would be what I consider an acceptable twist out for my party tonight."

"Nicole, are you saying you don't like my hair?" my voice cracked, and a tear grazed my eyes, ready to fall.

"Pudding Pop, that's not what I'm saying at all. I'm just saying your dress is beautiful, you're beautiful, and I want everything to be beautiful. I'm sure whatever you're going to do with your hair will be fine. Just make sure you're on time because remember this party that I'm working so hard to throw and that I've spent so much money on I'm throwing for you." Patting me on my shoulder, she turned and walked away, barking orders at the movers to hurry up and get off her lawn with all the boxes.

How could I forget. That's all she talked about for the past couple of weeks. It seemed like every phone call was about how she was throwing this party for me. It baffled me because the majority of the people that was invited were her friends, but I was sure the party was going to be nice. I was excited to meet the rest of my extended family.

I was looking forward to spending time with my greats. I hadn't had great grandparents on my mother's side only my uma and umpa. I missed them dearly. I only spoke to them a couple of times since they went back home to Ghana. My greats on my father's side were nice people. I felt lucky they were still vibrant enough for me to spend time with them and get to know them while they were alive and well.

I skipped up the backstairs and ran smack dead into Maria. "Hey, Maria," I said.

"Hey, Nina," she replied with a warm smile. I really liked Maria. She was kind and I felt sorry for her because it was only one of her and it was six of us. Maria was my new version of Ms. Alba, just younger and quieter. The thing that made me sad about Maria was that she felt more like staff whereas in my house, Ms. Alba felt more like family. I tried to get to know Maria, but she was always in a rush and appeared to be scared to talk.

I walked into my bedroom and found my little brother, Greyson, jumping from my love seat to my ottoman.

"Buddy, what are you doing?"

"I like your new chair, Nina, it's fun."

"Well, you can have fun on it as long as you don't hurt yourself."

"Greyson! Greyson!" I heard Nicole calling him from down the hall.

"Greyson, you better come here and let Maria bathe you so you can be ready for my party.

"Where are you, Greyson?"

"Uh oh, buddy, you better go. Seems like your mom is looking for you." I picked him up and put him down on the floor.

"Oh, man, I like hanging out in your room," Greyson

whined.

He walked out of my room with slumped shoulders and dragged his feet.

"Hey, buddy." He turned to look at me.

"When the party is over you can come back. You're welcome to hang out in my room any time you want, okay?"

"Okay, Nina." Greyson smiled, racing out the door and jump kicking the air.

"Stop running in this house, Greyson." Nicole enjoyed yelling demands and she was starting to irritate me.

I was no longer excited for this party. Instead of getting in the shower, I decided to work on my mother's mural.

"Hey, Mommy. I'm back." I extended my arms with the palms of my hands together. I split my dresses down the middle. I exposed a set of almond-shaped eyes, looking directly at me. The eyes were stunning; they were my mother's eyes. Working on them gently, I picked up my tools and start fading the blacks against the whites of the eyes. I was focused on the meticulous and tedious work, so time got away from me.

"I'm sorry, Mom. I have to leave for a little while but don't worry, I'll be back, and I'll finish working on your beautiful face." I kissed the wall then got dressed for the party.

When I entered the party, it was in full swing. There were

people talking and mingling while staff walked around, serving drinks and appetizers.

"Finally." Nicole startled me, walking up behind me. "Come here, there are some important people I would like for you to meet."

I looked through the crowd and I saw my greats, Diane, and Mario. I stepped away from Nicole and walked toward them with my arms open, ready to embrace them with a hug.

"You guys look so beautiful. I really missed you. What took you so long to come back and see me," I spoke in a sing song voice, sounding like a little girl.

"Oh, honey, we live about forty-five minutes away from here and we don't get out as much as we would like. We sure did miss you and we're happy you call us every so often, majority of our grands never call us, they never check in on us, and barely spend time with us anymore. I guess us old folks are played out."

"Grandma Diane, you and Pops are not played out. I love spending time with you and when I get my license and a vehicle, I'm going to make sure I come visit you as much as possible."

"When do you get your license? I heard that you've been taking classes," my grandpa asked.

"I take my test in two weeks. I'm so excited and I'm ready to drive."

Nicole walked up and inserted herself right between us.

"Why are you so excited to drive? It's not like you have a car, young lady."

My smile escaped my face, but I didn't respond. She was right; I didn't have a car. However, Riley had a car so I assumed that once I got my license, I would get a car as well. From Nicole's tone, it looked like it might not happen if she had anything to do with it.

"I'm sure you'll get a car, sweetheart. Every other kid in this household of age has one, so why not you." I fell in love with my Great Grandma Diane. She was a spitfire. She said what she meant, and she had no filter on what came out of her mouth.

"We will see. Nina, come on. Let me get you and everyone together and make an announcement introducing you to everybody." Nicole grabbed my arm. When I turned to go with her, my grands, Sabrina, and Richard, walked in and swooped me away. I squealed and greeted them, happy to have a distraction.

"Gather around everyone. I want you guys to meet our granddaughter. She just moved here from New York and her name is Santina. She is my son's first born and now she lives with us permanently. She goes by Nina, please make her feel welcome and come on up to her and introduce yourself as you guys make your way around the party. We absolutely love her, and we are so happy that she's here. Everybody raise your glasses and let's all say welcome to Nina"

"Welcome Nina!" everyone yelled at the same time except for Greyson.

"You're welcome, Nina," he said after everyone else.

I looked over, and Nicole was sitting down with a glass of

champagne. I wasn't sure, but I think my Grandma Sabrina stole her thunder. It was obvious she enjoyed all eyes on her and at this point, I didn't know who enjoyed it more, her or my Grandma Sabrina. They were both socialites while my preference was the opposite.

As more people gathered, a couple of my new friends from my new school arrived with their parents. I watched the different interactions, and most people were blown away by Nicole's beauty. She got compliments on her dress, the house, and her impeccable taste. She had on a beautiful necklace everybody kept raving about. She was stunning. Nicole ate up all the compliments. I could tell she loved the attention. I could see how she mesmerized my father. Nicole was 5'11," with bisque colored skin. Her hair was naturally curly in a short, tapered style that enhanced her high cheek bones and long slender nose. Nicole had greenish-blue eyes and was slim with perky 34D breasts. I was sure my dad paid for those since she went braless most times. Although she gave birth and bragged to me about how she breastfed her three kids, they stood at attention.

Nicole's laugh annoyed me. She was over the top, performing like a circus animal.

"Nina, darling, come over here and meet some of your father's employees. These people are very supportive of your father's business. Everyone this is our oldest daughter, Nina."

People spoke from all directions and all I could do was smile and say hello back. I felt like an item on display.

Riley, Ryan, and friends grabbed my arm, pulling me to a

quiet corner so that we could play a made-up game called *Guess Who.*

"Okay, Nina, try to guess who had a scandal in the church because they were sleeping with their landscaper," Riley whispered. I looked around at the people Nicole was talking to, but I couldn't imagine who.

"Is it her over there." I lifted my chin in the direction of a woman talking to Nicole. She looked a lot younger than her husband. I assumed if anyone was sleeping with the help it would be her.

"Nope, it was her husband," Riley said.

"Oh," I said with wide eyes. "You didn't mention that their landscaper was a woman? That's not fair."

"It is fair," Riley giggled. "Their gardener is not a woman." Riley raised her eyebrows, Riley pressed her lips together, and shook her head up and down.

"Oh, wow. It appears that our church has a lot going on."

"Yep," Riley said. "But he prayed it away with our deacon of a daddy, so I guess he's fine now."

We giggled and moved on to the next person. Before Riley gave me the scenario, I asked her about the group of white people that came through the door.

"Oh, they are not white. That's our two aunts and our three uncles."

"Oh," I said, shocked that they were related to me.

"Those are Daddy's brothers and their wives."

"Oh, that's Uncle Blaze, Uncle Ace, and Uncle Legend?" I quizzed, realizing that they looked paler than the pictures I saw of them.

"Yep. You know Grandma Sabrina is creole, right?"

"I knew she was something. I honestly thought she was biracial."

"No, she's black. She's from Louisiana."

"Ah," I said softly.

"Our dad is the only brownish one of the crew and even he is what our community considers beige."

"I see. Grandpa Richard is responsible for giving him that little bit of beige, but the color didn't reach the rest of them." Riley laughed at my response.

"Creole," I said under my breath, looking at my aunts and uncles who were walking toward me. My father and his brothers were all over six feet, so it looked like mountains were moving in my direction. I kept my feet planted with my hands clasped behind my back.

"Hey, Hey, beautiful," one of my uncles grabbed me up, lifting me to my tippy toes. They hugged me while analyzing my face like I was a rare artifact.

"Damn, she looks just like Ola with Santino's dimples," Uncle Legend said.

"You guys knew my mom?" I asked.

"Of course, we knew your mom, kiddo. Your dad was a fool for her back in the day."

I smiled from ear to ear. I wanted to ask a million questions, but Nicole ended that.

"Hey guys, I see you met your niece." Nicole eyes were glossed like she drank one too many cocktails and her hands were on her hips.

"Yeah, man, we were just saying that she looks a lot like her mom," my Uncle Blaze stated to his wife, ignoring Nicole.

"She's striking," his wife responded.

"Well, I'm not sure who she looks like, but she does have really thick nappy hair like her momma had." She placed her hands in my hair and scrunched her nose, acting like my hair stank. My twist out shorter with shrinkage since my hair was cut.

"I tried to get her to get a blow out or braid it, but she likes it like this," Nicole said, throwing her hands up and shaking her head.

My Uncle Legend broke the uncomfortable silence. "Well, I love her hair. I think it's cool."

"Thank you," I said with a shaky voice.

I walked away from them and ran up the back stairs. I didn't stop running until I got to my room. I slammed the door, tore off the ugly ass black dress, and cut it with my shears. I cried and stabbed the fabric, pretending it was Nicole. I went into my closet and continued to work on my mother's mural.

Delia Rouse

Chapter Fourteen

"**N**ina! Hey Nina! Wait for us!"

"Hey Ryan. Hey Riley. What are you guys up to?"

"We were looking for you. Where are you walking to?"

"Nowhere in particular. I like to go for walks along the property line because it's nice out here."

"Really?" Riley looked around. "It looks like nothing but a bunch of grass and bugs to me."

"I guess it's because I am from the city. I am so used to the sounds of cars honking, the train overhead, and people chattering twenty-four seven. I think it's nice to hear nothing. Just the silence of nature. It's peaceful."

"Yeah, I heard NY doesn't have any trees," Ryan quizzed.

"We have trees, silly. We just don't have as many as you guys do down here."

"Did you enjoy your party last night? Everybody was talking about you." Ryan smiled.

"Talking about me? Why? Was it my hair?"

Ryan and Riley looked at each other weird.

"What was wrong with your hair? Why would people be talking about that?" Ryan asked.

"I dunno." I felt self-conscious. I touched my hair. It wasn't curly and free flowing like Ryan and Riley's hair.

"What's wrong, Nina? Something tells me you didn't enjoy your own party."

"Well.......I felt different that's all."

"Why?" Ryan and Riley asked in unison.

"I guess because you guys all have the same parents and I have a different mom." I folded my hands over my chest, shrugged, then rubbed my arms like I was cold.

"Every time someone walked up to me, they would say, *'oh, so this is her? This is Santino's other daughter or wow she looks just like her dad but darker.'* It was annoying and made me feel weird."

"Well, don't be annoyed and you're not different. You just have to get to know everybody and since our family is so big it will take a while." Ryan rubbed my back, and I relaxed a little.

"The good thing is all of our cousins are younger than us and we lead the cousin pack!" Riley smiled and raised her fist in the air.

"I guess that would make sense since our dad is the oldest of his siblings," I said to them. We walked along the path then sat down at the small lake. "I know your mom meant well but…" I treaded lightly because I didn't want to offend them.

"We know she is a lot to take in but she's the best mom ever," Riley responded.

"Yeah, I think she was an actress in her previous life because she always on ten," Ryan laughed.

I decided to keep my thoughts to myself about how their mom hurting my feelings when she was talking about my hair. I wasn't sure they could relate because they had thick, wavy hair and although they were darker than their mom, they were still considered light-skinned.

"Nina, can I ask you a question?" Ryan made me nervous. I hoped it wasn't a question about Nicole.

"Give it to us straight. Are you happy here?"

I momentarily stopped breathing and looked at them. I wasn't sure if they saw the sadness in my eyes. I wanted to choose my words carefully because they had been so welcoming.

"Well, here's the truth. I'm happy that I met you guys and now have sisters. Back home, it was just me and my mom. I always thought I was the only child. I knew my dad had other children but since I've never met you guys, I just pushed it out of my mind. So, I am happy that we now know each other. But I do miss my mom and I know it's hard for you guys to understand because you still have both of your parents. But my mom was the greatest woman I knew, and she loved me so much."

"We understand, Nina." They hugged me and it made me feel good. I leaned into Riley and lingered on her shoulder.

"I guess I just feel different."

"Why do you keep saying that Nina?" Riley shifted, causing me to lift my head.

"I think it's because you guys look mixed, and I look like a black girl." I blew out a breath hard. There it was. I said it out loud.

"You think we look mixed?" Riley replied.

"I don't think we look mixed," Ryan said.

"I think our mom looks bi-racial, but I don't think we look mixed." Riley was pointing back and forth from her to Ryan.

"You're right, guys. I guess what I mean is when you look at us as a whole. For instance, if we took a family photo, I am the only dark skin person in the family. It seems apparent that I am an outsider."

"We don't care about that, Nina," Ryan replied.

"Yeah, we don't care about that, and you're definitely an insider," Riley repeated.

"We think you're beautiful. I wish I had brown skin like yours. I wish I had your dimples! We once overheard our dad talking to Uncle Legend and he was saying how beautiful your mom was and that she was a model too."

I smiled. I always loved hearing stories about my mom.

"We also heard that she was from Africa! Have you ever been to Africa, Nina?" Riley and Ryan eyes were wide with excitement.

"Yes. My grandparents still live there. My mom and I went a couple of times for the holidays. It's beautiful over there."

"We have always wanted to go to Africa!" Riley said.

"Hey, we should all go in a couple of years when we graduate!" Ryan was smiling wide, walking backwards in front of us then jumping up and down in the air like she had the best idea ever.

"Guys, I will tell you this. If you are serious and we do take a trip to Africa, I would ask my family if we could stay with them and I promise you, they would take good care of us and make sure we had a great time," I proclaimed.

"Well, I think it's settled. When we graduate high school, we are taking a sisters' trip to the motherland."

"Nina, I want to tell you something also. I know you said you feel different but please don't. You're not different because we have a different mom. I have a different dad. So, me and you are more alike than you think." Riley raised her eyebrows and tilted her head toward me.

I was stunned.

"Santino is not your dad?"

"No, he's not my real dad."

"Where is your dad?" I was very puzzled now because I saw pictures of my dad holding Riley as a baby.

"My dad is dead. I never met him. He was killed in a car accident before I was born."

I gasped, covering my mouth.

"I'm sorry, Riley."

"It's okay. Santino and my mom married when she was pregnant with me, so Santino is the only dad I know," Riley stated, hunching her shoulders and resumed our walk.

"What about your grandparents on your dad's side. Do you have any aunts or uncles?"

"I am not sure. I don't know anyone on my real father's side. The only family I claim on my dad's side is Santino's family."

I wasn't sure what to make of her not wanting to know her birth family. I would've had so many questions about them if I were in her shoes.

"I guess that is why Nicole told me I could call her mom a couple of weeks ago," I said to Ryan and Riley.

"Yeah, she wants us to be one big happy family," Ryan chuckled.

"I get it now. It's just a little different for me," I paused, trying to gather my thoughts.

"How is it different?" Ryan asked.

"It's different because I had my real mom all of my life until now and she will never be replaced." We turned around at the same time and I was startled. Nicole was standing right behind us.

"Ma, you scared us. What are you doing here?" Riley

asked.

"Taking my daily run and enjoying my property," Nicole said, smiling and pulling Riley in with one arm for a hug.

I wasn't sure how much she heard. I decided to extend an olive branch to Nicole and say something to her.

"Maybe we can run together sometimes."

"You couldn't keep up." Nicole glared coldly at me. She kissed her kids, waved goodbye, then proceeded with her run.

Chapter Fifteen

"Hey, Daddy, you took off today?" I placed my arms around his neck from behind and kissed him on the cheek. I was excited to see him. It surprised me how little time he spent in the house. I assumed I would see him more since we lived under the same roof. I craved nothing more than quality time and love from him.

"No, baby. When you own the company there is no such thing as taking off."

"Hmmm, well then I am not sure if I'll ever own a company. Can't you hire people to manage it the way we have hired help managing this house?"

"Technically, I run this house. I just have a little help,"

Nicole sneered. Once again, she popped up out of nowhere. I felt like this lady was fucking Houdini.

"Oh, hey, Nicole," I said while grabbing a seat.

"So, guys, I know I haven't been home a whole lot lately because business has been busy, but we are about to get even busier! I am going to have to do a lot of traveling in the next few months." Shit! I was hoping he would be home more, not less.

"Daddy, are you going to be able to come to my open house?"

"When is it again, Nina? I may not be able to make it, but Nicole will go." That was the last thing I wanted to hear right now.

"Nina, let your dad finish. It's rude to interrupt him." I looked at Nicole but didn't say a word.

"With that being said, guys, during your winter break I am taking the whole family on vacation to Jamaica!"

Cheers exploded from around the table. Me, Riley, and Ryan hugged each other while jumping up and down.

"Wow, I knew you guys would be excited, but this right here is ecstatic!"

"Guys, I just want to say that I'm so happy that my entire family is together. You guys are getting along so well. Nina, Riley, and Ryan and you seem to have gotten pretty close."

"Yes, Daddy, we have. We sleep over in Nina's room sometimes and sometimes she sleeps in our room. I also told her don't worry about not fitting in, that she fits in just fine," Riley said.

"Nina also made the volleyball team at school," Ryan blurted out. I sulked because I wanted to tell my dad myself.

"Is that right, Nina? That's amazing. You know the academy that you girls go to is a top-notch school for sports. Why didn't you tell me?" my father asked. I was perplexed because when had he been home long enough for me to tell him?

"Well, Daddy, I haven't seen you lately and I wanted to tell you in person instead of over the phone or by text message." This was the difference between him and my mom. My mom was completely involved in my life and there was not one thing that went on she wasn't aware of when it came to school.

"Did you make junior varsity or varsity?" he quizzed.

"Varsity!" I beamed proudly, showing all my teeth.

"My girl!" he screamed. It felt nice. I was finally getting my dad's attention.

"Riley made the team as well, honey," Nicole stated, making a sweeping motion with her hand over to Riley. She always had a way of dimming my light.

"Well, Daddy, I only made JV," Riley sulked.

"Well, that's good too, sweetie," he replied. "Now, let's talk about Jamaica!"

"I will carve out a week. I want to rent a private villa on a small island." My dad's hands were sweeping across the air dramatically. He had been married to Nicole way too long.

"Nicole, baby. Set it up."

"I'm on it, baby," she responded coyly, looking at him.

"Kids, I want you guys to pick two excursions that you want to do, and I'll have Maria set that up." Nicole was standing with her palms on the table. I was looking at her slender toned frame in her fitted tea length dress acting as if she paid for anything when she didn't work. The way she took ownership and passed the task on to Maria in the same sentence made me cringe. I wondered how my dad could be in a relationship with her and my mom in the same lifetime when they were polar opposites.

"Nina, Ryan let's plan a sleepover so we can discuss what excursions we want to do and what we are going to wear." Riley was hyped.

"Nina, have you ever been to Jamaica?" Nicole asked.

"No, ma'am, I haven't. I'm super excited," I responded.

"Good," my dad exclaimed. "Baby girl, this will be the first of many family vacations you will enjoy with us before you girls graduate and leave Nicole and I."

Nicole took her position as the trophy wife at the head of the table with my dad.

"I'll never leave you, baby," she said in a voice that was too sexy for me to witness.

"I know you won't, doll. But our babies will one day so make sure you make this an incredible vacation. Especially since it will be Nina's first vacation with us."

"I sure will." Nicole eyed me while pulling my dad's face close to hers and kissing his cheek.

Chapter Sixteen

T he first half of the school year went by fast. The academy was serious about their sports program. The volleyball tryouts and practice schedule were accelerated and more intense than what I was used to in New York. We practiced every day after school for three hours which had me getting home most nights after six. I didn't mind since my new home was just a house, there was no warmth, no random hugs or I love you's handed out and that was something that I missed. I craved the emotional connection but was also scared of it since it had a history of being snatched away from me multiple times and instantly.

First my mother was taken from me, then Ms. Alba and Teddy. There wasn't a warning, no slow illness, no time to make amendments, say I'm sorry, or I love you. They were just gone. It didn't smolder like a candle snuffer to a flame. It was more like blowing out a candle violently, splattering the wax everywhere. The remnant of that splatter was my life without Omalara Fondula Ayinde.

Loving on Greyson scared me but every time he saw me, he jumped into my arms, hugging me with his tiny arms which set my heart ablaze with warmth. Riley and Ryan were cool. They were into their boyfriends, designer clothes, and social life but we giggled and gossiped together which was our way of bonding. My time with my sisters was nice but nothing deep. My time with my baby brother was love, natural, untainted, and innocent.

I was looking forward to this family trip because it was close to my birthday, and I dreaded my birthday. The distraction would help me since my mother died a couple of days prior and since part of me died with her, I viewed my birthday as my death-day. I looked forward to the Caribbean food and spending time with the people since they had a similar culture to Ghana. The trip was coming up in less than seven days and Nicole had obliterated my dad's credit cards by the looks of all the stuff gathered in the bonus room for the trip. I rarely slept in my bed, which made Maria think I was great at keeping my room clean, but the truth was that I slept in my closet under my mother's mural most nights.

"Alright, girls, make sure you pick up panties and bras, toothbrushes, toothpaste, razors, lotion, and all the toiletries you will need for Jamaica. Get sunscreen and bug spray. Flip flops and whatever else." Nicole was giving us instructions although we had been planning for the last three weeks and we each had a meticulous list written out.

"Nicole, can I get a bathing suit?"

"Sure, Nina. Get whatever you need, honey."

Riley, Ryan, and I walked up and down each aisle in Target.

"What do you guys think of this bathing suit?" I asked.

"Too much material," Riley said, shaking her head back and forth.

"What about this one?" I picked up another one.

"No, here is one for you! This one is perfect; it would go great with your skin tone and your body type." Ryan held up a bunch of strings and placed it near my body.

"That's a bikini. I am not sure about a bikini, but that mustard yellow is stunning."

"We are wearing bikinis,'' Ryan stated, pointing at her and Riley.

"I know but I'm unsure if I want my booty hanging out. I'm way too self-conscious." I shook my head

"Nina, you play volleyball and practice five days a week. You don't have an ounce of body fat. If anyone could pull this bikini off, it is you."

"Ryan, how about we look for something with a little more material. I like full coverage bottoms."

"Okay, but you are way too young to be a prude."

"I wish I had the confidence you girls have. Oh, and I also want to find a nice cover up."

"Oh geez…. now we know you're a prude." Ryan and Riley laughed at me, and I joined.

"Guys, how did we end up with a full shopping cart basket worth of stuff?" The shopping cart was overflowing, and we had placed things on the bottom of the cart as well.

"It Jamaica, sis. We cannot have too much stuff," Ryan said.

"Ma, where you at. We are done. You want to meet us at the cash register?" Riley called Nicole. We needed her to pay for all the crap we piled into this cart.

"Okay will do." Riley disconnected the call.

"Ma said for me to put it on my card."

Her card? They have their own credit cards? I have been living with my new family for several months now and I am still learning something new every day.

"Let's go checkout."

"Is that Greyson?" Maria also had a shopping cart full of items and was trying to grab Greyson's hand.

"Greyson, come here, buddy," I called.

He ran toward me and jumped into my arms. "Why are you running around this store like a wild boy?" I kissed his chubby cheek.

"Because he is a wild boy," Riley said, rolling her eyes.

Maria walked up briskly, taking a deep breath.

"Hey, guys. I am happy you are here. This little guy almost got away from me."

Greyson was giggling and trying to run like it was a game.

"Where's Nicole?" I asked, looking around.

"She got the car service to drop her off at the salon so she can get herself prepped for your family vacation. If you guys are done, we can pay and leave. Our car is back and will drop us off and pick Nicole up later when she is done." I wasn't surprised because Nicole was not a hands-on mother.

Once we got home, we laid out all our clothes and played around with different looks. I didn't really know what it was like to go on vacation with a big family. My vacations were always just me and my mom.

"Nina, which outfit do you like best? The flowered romper short set or the two-piece skirt set?" Riley was stuck on a fashion choice.

"I think they are both beautiful, let's think about this.

Where would you wear the romper?"

"Good question, maybe to dinner or on an excursion."

"Okay and where would you wear the two-piece skirt set?"

"Hmmm," Riley pondered with her hand on her chin, looking at the outfits.

I tuned Riley out as thoughts ran through my head on how I secretly wished it was a father daughter trip with just me and him. I had so many questions that I had been scared to ask and wanted to use this vacation to at least scrape the topic of why he missed so many years from my life.

"Well, let me finish packing. In two days, we will be chilling on a beach drinking virgin Pina Coladas. We out, sis," Riley said, snapping me out of my trance.

"See ya, guys."

I closed my door. I wanted to work on the mural. I was almost finished with my mom's face and it was coming along beautifully. I thought I heard my dad calling my name, but I wasn't sure. I continued working on her jawbone and I heard my name again. *He must be home*, I thought. I covered the back wall and ran down the hall.

"Nina, come here please, baby." My dad paced the floor with his hands on his hips. I could tell he was angry. Nicole's face was beet red, and she was sniffling. I was concerned and prayed nothing happened to my great-grandparents.

"Daddy, what's wrong? What happened? Is my grandma and grandpa okay?" His pacing back and forth made me nervous.

"Nina, I'm so damn angry right now!" "What

did I do, Daddy? I didn't do anything."

"I know you didn't, baby. None of this is your fault." He

shot daggers at Nicole.

"What happened, Daddy?" I wrung my ashy hands until

they burned. I wanted him to spit it out.

"Nina," Nicole said through tears. "When I was going

through the itineraries and gathering all the documents, I realized

that you do not have a passport."

"Nicole, how is that possible? I know I have a passport."

What type of bullshit is she trying to pull?

"Nicole, how did you buy plane tickets if you didn't already

have Nina's passport?" my dad questioned.

"Yeah."

"I took pictures of her passport on my phone when we went

to her mother's funeral. I was gathering all of her paperwork and I

like to have digital copies but then we decided to let her stay with

Alice and since we were not sure if she would live with her

grandparents in Africa or with Alice, I didn't bring her social

security card, birth certificate, or passport back with us."

Nicole was crying but I felt no remorse for her. I wanted my dad to

tear into her lies.

"Nicole, how in the world could you let something like this

happen?" My dad's voice elevated.

"I allow you to stay home and not work so that you can

manage our family and our home. I pay for you to have an assistant because you said you needed help. I pay for car service because driving with the kids was stressful, everything I do is so that you can have an easier life. The only thing I ask of you is to make sure things run smoothly at home. You know I work to pay for all of this, and I depend on you to keep the family straight and it seems like you can't even do that!"

"What's going on down here?" Riley and Ryan ran to the room when they heard the commotion.

"Honey, I will file for an emergency passport! If we pay the expedited fee the passport will come in twenty-four to forty-eight hours. She's not a first-time applicant and since it's a renewal it can come faster." Nicole was talking fast like a salesman making a pitch.

"Fuck!" my dad knocked a paperweight off his desk in his bedroom. He hit it with such force, he knocked a dent in the wall. We jumped.

"That's it. We are cancelling this vacation. How in the hell can we go on a family vacation when all my family can't go? Damn, Nicole!"

"Wait, we do not have to cancel. Everything is paid for. When Nina's emergency passport comes in, she can fly—"

My dad cut her off and turned around swiftly, looking at Nicole. She looked like she saw a ghost. Her eyes were wide. She braced herself for a blow to the jawbone, which I wished I could deliver.

"Are you about to suggest that she flies to another country

alone?"

"Of course not, baby. I was going to say she can fly to Jamaica with Maria; I am sure she used to fly with her nanny, Alice, when she was home living in New York right, Nina?"

I didn't acknowledge her. I stared straight ahead at the wall with tears running down my face.

"Alba," I whispered.

"What?" Nicole asked, walking toward me.

"Alba."

"Who is Alba?"

"Alba is my nanny's name who you keep referring to as Alice. Her name is Alba!" I yelled at the top of my lungs. Nicole stepped back, and all eyes were on me. Something deep inside of me told me that Nicole never planned on taking me on this trip and something even deeper inside told me that my dad was a dummy if he couldn't see through his lying wife.

"This is so messed up." Ryan ran out of the room crying.

"Why is everyone attacking me. I try so hard to make sure Nina is comfortable and I depended on Maria to assist me in this, and she let me down which caused me to let you guys down."

"Maria! Maria, get up here right now please!" Nicole walked to the entryway of her room when she saw Maria coming out of Greyson's room.

"Yes, Mrs. Wellington?" Maria asked in a polite tone.

"Maria, how could you miss the fact that we didn't have Nina's passport? I asked you to assist in booking this trip."

"Huh? Mrs. Nicole you said—"

"Maria, now you will have to fix this." Nicole cut her off before she could finish. Maria looked confused and baffled like she had no idea what Nicole was talking about.

"If Nina can't go then I will stay home with her," Riley said, wrapping her arms around my neck. I appreciated the gesture and wished it was my dad who was saying these words instead of Riley. It wouldn't have been so bad if they all went to Jamaica and he and I was left home to spend quality time together. Instead, my dad answered a call and appeared distracted.

"No," Nicole said firmly.

"Nina is going. Riley you are going. We are all going on this trip. Nina will be there twenty-four hours after us. Maria will make sure of that. Right, Maria!" Nicole demanded.

"Yes. Yes, Mrs. Wellington," Maria said with her head hung low.

Disconnecting his phone, my dad finally jumped back into the conversation.

"Maria, you have been with our family for a long time, and I am disappointed that you dropped the ball on something as major as this. I need to run into the office for an hour or two." My dad brushed past Maria and kissed my forehead. "So sorry, baby, but we will fix this, okay?" He didn't wait for a response and was out the door.

"I'm going to go lay down." I broke out of Riley's embrace and went to my room, locking the door. I ran into my closet, pulled my clothes off the hangers, slid down on the floor by my mother's mural, and cried.

"Mommy, I wish I could be with you," I said, talking to the mural. I felt defeated. I grabbed the throw off the chaise lounge in my closet and curled up like a fetus. I cried myself to sleep on my closet floor under my mother's face.

Delia Rouse

Chapter Seventeen

T he line had been drawn in the sand once I never made it on the family vacation. I got Nicole's memo loud and clear. My dad started out calling me every couple of hours with ways that he was getting my passport situation corrected so that I could meet them in the Caribbean.

By day two, I realized it was not going to happen and I stopped answering his calls. I simply sent a text response. *Enjoy your family. I'm fine. The Greats said I could hang with them this week.* I cut off my phone. There was nothing that could be said to erase the resentment I felt toward him. I knew this was all Nicole. I had no idea why, but that lady didn't like me and while she was cordial, she was always very curt, short, overly nice, and sarcastic. I was beginning to think she may have been bi-polar but then I thought no because her foolish behavior was only directed toward me.

I would turn on my phone because of urges to check Riley and Ryan's Instagram, which made me feel worse because the family selfies and beautiful photos of the island made me resentful. Jealousy overtook me because they went from '*if Nina can't go we don't want to go*' to having the times of their lives and not thinking about me at all. I went back to that empty feeling of having something snatched away from me and felt like God teased me with the idea of being a part of my father's family.

Spending time with my Greats was nice but it didn't stop the pain and the emptiness that I felt inside. My tears still swallowed me up at night and I only found comfort in sleeping. My dreams felt so real when I saw my mom; I could hear her voice and smell her perfume and she was real while my eyes were closed. I decided I wanted to sleep forever but my Greats choose a different path for me.

My Greats were perceptive and when they noticed I was sleeping all day, they forced me to get out of bed. Their instincts led them to conversations with me about God and living a life of service.

"Nina, I want you to have faith that God has a plan for your life. He wouldn't put more on you then you were able to handle. I know it's tough, Nina, but you have so much life ahead of you," my grandma would say to me as she allowed me to cry in her arms some nights.

Since that week, I spent the weekends with my Greats which included volunteering at a community center they owned and going to church with them on Sundays. Weekends with my Greats helped me push through difficult weeks. Church services filled me up and gave me the fuel I needed and just when my tank was almost empty, it was Friday and Bernard would drop me back off to my great grandparents. My soul was replenished by the end of our time together.

"Grandma Diane, tell me what my dad was like when he was a little boy."
She smiled and sat back, rocking in her chair. She closed her eyes as if she was trying to remember what my dad was like when he was a young boy.

"I can tell you that he was a bad ass kid," my grandpa
jumped right in, recalling my dad's
behavior when he was younger.

"Your dad was a busy kid he always had big dreams and
sort of remind me of Greyson,
just busy," my grandma added.

"You know, I think with him being the oldest of four boys
your dad was always

responsible. He felt like he had to look out for the younger boys and he always worked hard. He was our first grandson," my grandma beamed.

"Yeah, remember when he worked the paper route?" my grandma said, looking up and shaking her finger in the air.

"Yep, what about when he worked part-time at the corner store?" my grandpa said.

"Your dad has been working for as long as I can remember. Poor thing. He always felt he had to help out I guess because your Grandma Sabrina had so many kids back-to-back her hands were full. Your Grandma Sabrina and your Grandpa Richard were struggling when they were first married and so there was no such thing as hired help or a nanny or babysitter, they had to figure it out themselves. They were so young with a house full of kids."

"I'm just curious as to know more about my dad. He works so much and even though I've been here a year-and-a-half I don't feel like I really understand what type of person he is. It seems that every time I try to go to get close to him it fails. I know he has other kids he shares his time with but sometimes I feel invisible."

"Honey, you should never feel invisible," my grandmother said, rubbing my back and placing her cheek on mine as I sat on the floor in front of her.

"Yeah, it sucks, and I really was sad about it, but you know something, just like I'm trying to get to know my dad, I'm trying to get to know my great-grandparents too. And I am so upset that I hadn't met you guys sooner. I would've loved spending a week or two each summer with you." I rubbed my grandpa's knee and leaned against my grandma's leg. I was serious about that statement; I loved them.

"Well, honey, you are the first because out of all the grands or great grandkids that we have none of them really spends that much time with us anymore. I guess they're too busy with their fancy lives." My grandpa sounded a little upset when he said that.

"I enjoy hearing about your lives when you were young. What made you guys open up a community center?"

"We noticed that kids needed something to do and a safe place, especially the ones whose parents worked, not all kids have a nanny or two parent home. A lot of kids are home alone, which leaves them more time to be in the streets and to get into trouble, so we wanted to do something to help the kids in our community." My grandpa was proud.

"Grandpa, what made you guys buy that building?"

"Well, we had the building for over twenty-five years. What year was it that we bought that building, Diane?" Grandpa Mario's brows furled as he tried to remember the year.

"We bought that building many years ago when we got a settlement check from an accident. We had a sum of money, and we didn't know what to do with it. We also had a bunch of grandkids and great-grandkids so we figured we would have a place for them to go and have fun, especially since they never came and visited us."

"We had to do some repairs and we did a lot of fundraising. We got a couple of computers and partnered with some local churches, boy scout and girl scout troops, got a few volunteers and it's been a life saver for a lot of kids."

"I think it's such a great idea and I think that's honestly what keep you guys young. I enjoy the community center I think it's a fun place to be."

"We're happy that you visit as much as you do, and we are so glad that you have participated in the tutoring program because we need more young people like you. Now, if you can get your sisters, Ryan and Riley, to help out that will be awesome."

"I asked but they weren't interested honestly we had grown really close at one point but then after Jamaica something happen although I wasn't there, I feel like we became disconnected once they got back. I'm not sure anymore. I try not to worry about it. The community center helps me keep my mind off things, that and volleyball is what keeps me going."

"Is that what keeps you going? Or is it that boy, Dylan, that's been sniffing around you at the local community center? I'm old but I know when a little boy is sniffing around and interested in a beautiful girl." My grandpa looked at me over his glasses.

"What are you talking about, Grandpa? Grandma, what is Grandpa talking about?" I said, smiling.

"You know exactly what he's talking about, Nina. I've seen that boy too, it's not that much tutoring in the world, plus Dylan seems pretty smart so yeah, he's sniffing around you." I threw my head back and laughed at them. They were sharp as a tack, nothing got by them. Truth be told, I had a crush on Dylan, and we had been talking for weeks. I'm glad that my grandparents thought he was polite and liked him. It allowed me to spend more time with him. I reflected back to when Dylan and I first met.

"Turn the rope in circles Ciara just like Kandace is doing." I was teaching girl scout troop 1520 how to jump Double Dutch so that they could earn their athletic badge. The group of 11-year-old girls were struggling to catch the rhythm of the ropes.

"Can you show us how to jump in again, Nina?" a girl named, Kiana, asked.

"Sure thing, just turn your arms in huge circles and listen to the click clack sound of the ropes hitting the floor. When the rope closest to you goes up, you jump into the center of the rope and find your cadence."

I took a moment to find good timing and looked at the wired ropes, waiting on the perfect moment to jump in. It seemed like a small crowd gathered as I lifted my feet and jumped effortlessly, turning around looking at one rope turner then to the other to make sure they saw my form. While I jumped, I heard some of the girls squeal with excitement. My legs got tired and before they tripped me up in the rope, I stopped jumping by stepping on the rope when it looped around, which prevented it from popping my leg.

"Whoa," one girl yelled as the girls clapped when I finished.

"I wanna try next," another girl called out.

"Sure thing but let's go grab some water first and I'll make sure all of you alternate trying to turn and jump, let's take a ten-minute break and come back." I smiled at the girls and turned to get some water when a tall, brown skinned boy with piercing eyes handed me a cold bottle of water.

"Thanks." I blushed.

"You welcome. Where you learn how to jump like that?" he asked.

"Brooklyn," I stated proudly.

"Oh yeah, you think you could teach me?" the tall boy said, smiling with his hands in his jean pockets. He was sagging a little but not enough to be deemed disrespectful. I saw a piece of pink bubble gum dancing in his mouth and watched him lick his lips.

"Are you trying to earn a girl scout badge too?" I asked, smiling.

"Nah, I'll save the badges for the little ones you teaching."

"Well, then no. I can't teach you how to jump."

"That's cold, BK" I was baffled. I tilted my head to the side.

"Who's BK?" I quizzed.

"You. You from Brooklyn, right?"

"Yeah, but my name is Nina," I said, downing my water.

"Nina's a pretty name but Imma call you BK."

"Oh, really and what should I call you?"

"My name is Dylan but you can call me your boyfriend. You better get back to it, looks like your girls are waiting on you." Dylan grabbed my water bottle and drank the rest of it as he walked off.

"Speaking of the community center, let's go ahead and get down there so we can get ready for the seminar we have set up discussing our new read a book challenge for the children," my grandpa said, snapping me out of my thoughts. He was leaning on the arms of the chair for support and reached for his cane.

"I wish we would've had this community center when our grandchildren were younger. Lord knows your father could have used an outlet to hang out at maybe have some little girls that he was sniffing after something to smarten him up that way he wouldn't have been trapped into thinking he was the father of a child that wasn't his and he might have married different had he known better." I was shocked by what my grandfather said. Riley told me that when they met my dad accepted her mom being pregnant, but it looks like he was also a victim of *Mrs. Nicole.* I was even more intrigued about who my dad was, and I wanted more information to figure him out.

Chapter Eighteen

I was placing some flyers on the counter at the center about an upcoming book fair. The walls were painted a vibrant orange, red, and yellow. The walls had paintings of children without faces. It screamed warm and inviting for the youth. There were also several small classrooms.

"Nina, come here. I have somebody that I want you to meet," my Grandma Diane yelled.

"Who is it, gramps?" I didn't look up from what I was doing, assuming it was a parent thanking me for tutoring their kid.

"It's a friend of mine that helps around the community center. She comes a couple of times per month. Her name is

Bryce."

I walked with my grandmother to meet Bryce. I was not interested. I had my eyes on Dylan who just walked through the door with his pants slightly sagging and wearing Timberland boots.

"Bryce. This is my great granddaughter, Nina."

"Hello, Nina, nice to meet you. I've heard so many great things about you. Your great grandparents talk about you all the time. How are you enjoying North Carolina?" She extended her hand for me to shake.

Bryce was absolutely stunning. She looked like she was in her late twenties, 5'9," slim but curvy. Bryce's hair was long and thick. Her mahogany skin tone glistened.

"Are you ok, Nina?" my grandma asked.

"I'm sorry, forgive me for staring. You're so beautiful." I blushed.

"Awe, Nina. That's very kind of you. I think you're stunning as well."

It felt good to receive a compliment. I haven't had a genuine compliment since my mom died. I was intrigued with this Bryce woman. I wanted to know everything about her. What she did? How often she came to the community center? How long she would stay? If she had children? If she was married? I was obsessed. I yearned for a connection.

"Your great grandma tells me your mom was from Africa. Have you ever been to Africa?"

"Yes, yes, I have. My grandparents currently live there so

me and my mom used to go every couple of years."

"That's on my bucket list. I am obsessed with trying to get to giraffe manor. I plan to make a trip within the next couple of years." When Bryce smiled, her teeth were like white chicklets.

"I have plenty of family that currently lives there, so when you're ready you let me know or just take me with you." I laughed but I was serious.

"Let's shake on it. You got yourself a deal. I'm gonna hold you to this, Nina. I am very serious about visiting Africa."

"Ok, I believe you. I'm gonna hold you to those plans too," I said, pointing and giving her an exaggerated handshake.

"Do you ever wrap your hair in those beautiful head wraps? Do you know what tribe your family belongs to or what your tribal colors are? What about those beautiful outfits? Do you have any of those?" Bryce shot off several questions, but I didn't mind. It was nice that someone took interest in my culture.

"Unfortunately, I do not. Most of the things that I had representing my country was lost in a moving truck accident when my things were being transported from my home in New York to North Carolina."

"I have not had an opportunity to embrace my culture or learn how to wrap my hair. When my mom tried to teach me before she passed, I was insecure about wearing head wraps to school. Now, I wish I would've listened to her." My stomach felt queasy, and I was becoming emotional.

"Well, Nina, anytime you want to learn we can always

YouTube it. We can go to the fabric store and buy fabric and practice ourselves. I can definitely help you learn how to wrap your head," Bryce offered.

"I also have some close girlfriends who are Nigerian. I'm not sure what country your family is from, but they would love to show you how to wrap your hair or take you to the local African market here in Raleigh. Just let me know if you're interested."

"Bryce, can we exchange numbers? I'm definitely interested; it would make me feel closer to my mom."

"Absolutely, here take my card. My cell phone number is on it. You can call or text me anytime."

"Let me get to my book reading session. It was so nice to meet you, Nina. I look forward to us exploring your culture together. Mrs. Diane, will I be in classroom one?"

"Yes, dear," my grandma confirmed.

Bryce hugged us and then disappeared into the classroom.

"Alright, Nina. It seems like that went well. I knew Bryce was great."

"Grandma, that went better than well. She was so nice. Thank you so much for introducing me to her. She is so pretty too."

"You have been with us almost every weekend which we love. I had the feeling that you felt detached and isolated from your family at home from the conversations that we had, so I wanted to make sure I got you in contact with someone who could be like a mentor. Bryce is amazing. She's headed in the right direction, and she has a great head on her shoulders."

I hugged my grandma so tight; I thought she was going to burst. She gave me what I needed when I needed it without me even having to ask. That's the type of love I was used to and that's the type of love my mom always told me I deserved.

"Hey, Bryce. Hey, Mrs. Wellington. How's everybody doing?"

"Hey Dylan, how's it going?"

"It's going pretty well. Have you seen my tutor yet?"

"No, he hasn't gotten here yet, but I am sure you two will find something to chat about until he gets here." My grandma smirked at me then walked away.

I was excited to see Dylan. Me and him had become fond of each other. He was my secret. I hid him from my family because they didn't deserve a piece of what made me happy. We spent most of our time together on the weekends. My Greats had a furnished basement where we would hang out. Since they went to bed early, I slipped Dylan in some nights. Dylan was a year older than me and was being raised by a single mom. We talked often about our experiences with our moms and that connected us more. Dylan's mom worked twelve hour shifts at a hospital, which left Dylan home alone a lot.

One night, I slipped him into my Greats house through the basement door and he was visibly upset. His mother couldn't buy concert tickets to see his favorite rapper because her check was short and after paying her bills there wasn't enough left for the tickets.

"Yo, I never ask my mom for shit and the one thing I ask her for, and she promises to me and then flakes," Dylan whispered as his eyes watered. I looked away, not wanting him to feel embarrassed.

"When's the concert?"

"In two weeks at the Walnut Creek Amphitheater."

"That's the new outdoor theater in Southeast Raleigh, right?"

"Yeah." Dylan was sitting on the couch with his head hanging and his hands clasped between his legs.

"You think she could give you twenty dollars?" I asked.

"BK, what twenty dollars gonna do? Those tickets way more than twenty damn dollars. I got twenty dollars on me right now."

"Okay, keep that twenty bucks. I have an idea. We going to that concert."

Dylan scrunched his brows and twisted his lips.

"Yeah, whatever, BK."

Two weeks later, Dylan was picking me up in his Honda Accord. I had my huge volleyball duffle bag on my shoulders.

"Yo, we running away together or something?" Dylan

asked, smiling.

"You wish. We going to the Amphitheater," I stated, buckling my seatbelt. Dylan's eyes widened in shock.

"BK, you got me fucking tickets to see my man, Wiz, tonight!" Dylan voice elevated.

"Nah, my pockets not set up for purchases like that." I laughed.

"Then why we going over there than instead of chilling here?" Dylan frowned.

"Boy, drive. You asking too many questions. You'll see."

Dylan stared at me for a couple of seconds, shook his head, and started driving.

We paid the twenty dollars to get into the park. Once we got in and parked, I reached inside my duffle bag and pulled out fried chicken wrapped in foil that my Grandma Diane made along with sliced bread, drinks, hot sauce and snacks. We sat in the parking lot alone after droves of people went inside and listened to the concert from the car. Although we couldn't see anything, we heard everything, and Dylan sang every song and even got out the car to dance.

"Get out the car and dance with me, pretty lady." He grabbed my hand and we danced, having fun like the goofy teenagers we were. Dylan twirled me around and pulled me close to his face, gripping the sides of mine gently. It was a soft lingering peck on the lips that sent shockwaves through my body. Something happened below and I couldn't explain it, but whatever it was it had my underwear wet. My chest was rising up and down, showing my nervousness. The intensity in Dylan's stare made me feel like he was looking into my soul. He kissed me again, parting my lips with his tongue and I accepted it. I followed his lead because I wasn't sure what to do so I turned my head because I was embarrassed. He nuzzled his head into my neck. I looked up into the night's sky and saw a shooting star. I thought of my mother and pulled myself into Dylan's chest, allowing the overwhelming feeling of happiness to swallow me up in this moment.

When Dylan dropped me off to my Greats, he asked if he could come in. I was scared shitless. I wanted to say yes but I knew what would happen if I said yes. His eyes told me. I really needed my mom in this moment. I didn't know what to do.

"Dylan, tonight I wanted you to have a great time. I knew it wasn't the same as being inside the venue but..." I spoke in a shaky voice.

"I did. It was better than being inside the concert." Dylan was out of the car opening my car door and pulling me out. He pulled me close to him and hugged me tight.

Shit, I can feel his dick on my stomach.

"BK, can I come in?"

I took a quick breath and shifted my weight from one leg to another. I squeezed my eyes shut and felt his hands rubbing the nape of my neck with gentle strokes up and down. I looked up to the sky and bit my lip. I saw another shooting star.

"Yes," I whispered.

"Let me go in first and make sure my Greats are straight. Let them know I am home and see them off to bed."

"Alright."

That night, on the basement floor, I lost my virginity. It hurt like hell, and I bled some, but Dylan was patient and told me it would feel better. The act itself was not great but the closeness I felt to Dylan after allowing him access inside of my body made it special.

"BK, I have to get home before my mom gets in," Dylan whispered in my ear then sucked on my earlobe.

"I know," I said disappointed. I wished I could stay in these feelings forever.

"I love you, BK. Today was so perfect."

"It was."

"Imma call you later on tonight. Keep your phone close so you can answer. I'll text first."

I smiled and felt relieved to extend my time with him as long as I could whether in person or on the phone.

This started an ongoing weekend ritual. Dylan was right. The sex did get better.

I tried to spend a day or two during the week at the

community center if Bernard was available. Since I needed sixty driving hours logged in order to get my license it was always an excuse to drop in at the community center. Today, when Bernard picked me up from practice, I asked if I could drive out and he agreed. Bernard was awesome with helping me learn how to drive. It was another thing I just assumed that my dad would teach me but of course he didn't have the time. I ran smack dead into Dylan when I pulled up to the community center. I smiled and he pulled me into a hug.

"What time does your game start tomorrow? This is the first game of the season, isn't it?" Dylan asked me, smiling, and rubbing his chin.

"We play at 5:30. Yes, it's the first game."

"Are you nervous?"

"A little bit, but I plan to stay focused and do the best that I can."

"Do you think your parents and your siblings will come to watch you play?"

"Nah. My dad most likely has to work; my stepmother could care less, and my siblings probably will be hanging out with their boyfriends or shopping or doing something else that they're interested in. I don't know what's going on, I'm just not close to them at all. I was close to my sisters when I first moved here, but something changed, and they got distant. It doesn't feel like a family. I'm making the most of my life here with my Greats, spending time at the community center and playing volleyball. At this point, all I want to do is go to school, graduate, and move away to college somewhere far… very far."

"Damn, BK, that's kinda sad. You got this whole big family and it's like you're alone."

"Bingo. You pretty much summed up my life."

"Well, you know you have me. I'm gonna try and make sure I see you play a couple of games this season. Send me your schedule."

"Oh, you don't have to do that, Dylan. You don't have to spend your money coming to watch me play."

"It sounds like you don't want me there."

"I would love to have you there. Don't be silly. Here, I just sent you the schedule so now I expect to see you at a game or two."

"Alright, let's get to it. It looks like my tutor just walked through the door now. I'll talk to you when the hour is up, ok?"

"Ok, happy tutoring." I smiled until he was out of sight then I panicked. I knew Riley had mentioned Dylan's name before, so I hoped he didn't see her at the game and find her more appealing than me. My insecurities and possessiveness kicked in instantly.

Chapter Nineteen

The gym was loud, and the stands were filled with people holding small, navy-blue pom poms. I looked into the stands and saw my Grands and Bryce. I was so excited that they decided to watch my first game of the season. I hoped I played well. It felt good to have some support.

"N. I. N. A. Show them how well you can play."

"N. I. N. A. Show them how well you can play."

"N. I. N. A. Show them how well you can play."

Bryce was in full cheerleader mode. I wondered if she was a cheerleader in high school or college. My Greats sat beside her, pumping their fists in the air. I was used to having the stands empty when it came to loved ones supporting me. I didn't know how to act with my own private audience. I looked across the gym and saw Dylan walking through the door.

The final buzzer rang. We slaughtered the other team, beating them in three straight sets. I had several kills. I was on fire. I wasn't sure if it was because I had family in the stands watching me or if I channeled my frustration of my emotionally detached dad and overbearing, hateful ass stepmother out on the volleyball court.

"Wow, Nina, you were amazing. You had a great game."

"Thank you so much, Grandma Diane. Thank you guys for coming. Thank you, Grandpa Mario. Bryce, thank you so much for coming. It was so much fun to have people in the crowd cheering for me. Dylan, I can't believe you made it." When I hugged Dylan, all eyes were on us.

"So, we all came to watch you play and this chump is the only one that gets a hug." My grandpa was laughing with his palms up in the air.

"Grandpa, I'm sweaty and stinky. I didn't wanna hug you and mess up your nice clothes. I knew Dylan wouldn't care."

"Well, we don't care neither. You better come give us a hug too." Bryce had her arms opened wide.

"Nina, do you need a ride home?" my greats asked.

"Grandma Diane, is it okay if Dylan takes me home? We wanted to stop by and get ice cream on the way and I know it's a little bit of a drive from my house to yours."

"I don't mind at all. You just make sure you get her home safely, young man." My grandma pointed in Dylan's direction.

"Absolutely. It was nice seeing you guys again." Dylan shook my grandpa's hand, hugged my grandma, and waved goodbye to Bryce. He walked with me to the locker room and waited for me to shower and then off to get ice cream we went.

"Wow, this ice cream shop full. I think everybody who played this game came for ice cream." I was disappointed it was crowded.

"That's alright, we can wait. Are you in a rush to get home?"

"Is that a trick question? You know I am never in a rush to get to my house."

"Does that mean you wouldn't mind if I took you back to my house?"

The uncertainty in Dylan's voice made me blush. I loved the fact that he didn't assume because he was a nice-looking guy that I would go along with whatever he said. He always seemed unsure of himself, which made me feel better about being unsure of myself. I guess we were too unsure people who really liked each other.

"Is your mom still at work?"

"Yeah, she picked up some extra shifts for extra money."

Although Dylan was my first real boyfriend, having sex with him felt natural. I felt like he cared about me and he often asked how I felt, knowing the situation I lived in at home. Nicole was so self-absorbed and mean. My dad lived at his job and was so out of touch from the household, so no one noticed my absence. Riley and Ryan were obsessed with their boyfriends. Greyson was running Maria ragged and as long as Nicole had a bottle of wine; my dad's black card and no kids bothering her, she didn't care about anything.

On the drive to Dylan's house, I licked my ice cream cone aggressively trying to prevent it from melting.

"Damn, BK, you going to work on that ice cream cone," Dylan snickered, raising his brows up and down.

"I'm practicing," I said. Dylan head snapped back as he laughed.

"You can't say shit like that to me while I'm driving, BK. I almost ran off the road."

Dylan's house was modest compared to mine. I spent most of my time in his room so that nothing in his house was out of place when his mom came home. Pictures of Dylan from birth to present day was on display everywhere, showing that he was his mother's only child. His father lived with his new family, which made our connection to each other strong. I had lived the very same life before my mother passed.

"Ah, you always throw me off guard when you flip me over

on top," I squealed, giggling, and laughing in Dylan's ear.

"It's fun when you're on top," Dylan whispered, squeezing my butt cheeks.

I was in my groove, bouncing up and down on Dylan's manhood when the lights flicked on.

"What are you doing? Get your fast tail ass out of my house, young lady."

"Ma, what are you doing home?"

"Don't ask me what I'm doing home! I live here, boy." Dylan's mother was yelling and screaming like a madman.

I was mortified. I grabbed my clothes and tried to put them on as fast as possible. I wanted to run out the door but realized Dylan had drove. I had no way to get home.

"Mom, can I at least drop Nina off at home? She has no way to get home," Dylan pleaded while snatching the sheet from the floor to cover up.

"Nope, that won't be necessary. How about we'll call her parents and let them come pick her up. That way we can all have a conversation."

I felt a sense of doom. Calling Nicole was the last thing I wanted her to do. I knew she would run as fast as she could and tell my dad and I didn't want anything to strain our already fragile relationship more. I had screwed up big time.

Chapter Twenty

My mother always taught me that as long as she was living and breathing that I better not had ever disrespect an adult and if an adult was mistreating me to let her handle them. The only exception to this rule was an adult violating me in some way. In that case my mom always gave me full permission to show the fuck out and then tell her so that she could show the fuck out.

I was at an impasse in this moment because Dylan's mother was demanding my parents' number. I cared about Dylan, and I didn't want to disrespect his mother and most importantly, I didn't want to disrespect my mother, so I caved and gave her Nicole's number.

The moment I saw Nicole's white BMW 7 series pull up to Dylan's house I wanted to flee. I went to climb into the back seat while Nicole had words with Dylan's mom at the door.

"Do I look like Bernie to you?" Nicole asked.

"No," I responded

"Well, get your fast ass in the front seat then," she spewed.

"Ha ha," Nicole chuckled. I looked over and she was smiling and shaking her head from side to side. She slapped her hand on her steering wheel and drove in silence for several minutes before she started her verbal assault.

"Your dad is still out of town on business but when he calls me to check in tonight, I wonder how he will feel when he learns that his precious first-born daughter is fast and fresh."

I was so still; I thought my heart stopped. I said nothing. I looked straight ahead and prayed she drove faster so I could get out of the car and talk to my mother's mural.

"What do you have to say for yourself?"

"Nothing."

"Figures. Your dad has you all wrong. I knew from the moment I saw you that you would bring discord into my home."

"What?" I said, stunned.

"You heard me. I do not need my daughters persuaded by you and your behavior."

"How can that happen. I barely talk to your daughters. You

made sure of that." Nicole's head snapped and her face flushed red.

"What did your ungrateful ass just say?"

"Ungrateful? Ungrateful for what?"

"Excuse me, we provide a roof over your head, food in your stomach, and the best education that money can afford!"

"You don't provide me with shit! My father provides both me and you with all of those things and that is the absolute least he can do since he did create me! My mom didn't get pregnant by herself, and she damn sure didn't carry me for nine months, give birth to me, and anticipate that I would be neglected most of my life by my father because he married someone as selfish as you."

The car barely came to a complete stop before I jumped out the car like the seats were on fire.

"Nina," Nicole called me, seething.

"Nina, don't you walk your ass away from me!" Nicole screamed.

I kept walking until I was in the house, up the stairs, and in my room. I slammed my door and locked it then went into my closet and locked that door. I called Bryce and she talked me off the ledge and promised that she would check on me in the morning.

"Thank you for picking me up, Bryce. I didn't know who

else to call."

"Nina, you're a smart girl. What were you thinking by having sex in Dylan mom's house then starting a fight with your stepmom?" The disappointment on Bryce's face was too much for me to bear. I avoided eye contact with her and looked out the window.

"Are you on birth control, Nina?"

"No ma'am."

"Please tell me you guys used a condom."

"Yes, we did."

She pulled the car over and cut the engine. I felt humiliated and embarrassed; I couldn't face her.

"Nina, look at me."

Bryce rubbed my left shoulder as they jolted up and down from crying.

"Nina, don't cry. Having sex is natural. It's just something that comes with heavy consequences if you're not careful. I'm not upset with you and I'm happy you felt comfortable enough to call me. I don't agree with you disrespecting his mother's home or arguing with your stepmom, but we have all made some questionable decisions. Hell, I made one 2 days ago and he will not stop calling my damn phone."

Bryce poked my shoulder and it made me laugh.

"What makes Dylan so special? Tell me about him."

"Well, he pays attention to me. He treats me nicely and he tells me I'm smart and pretty."

"Anything else?"

"He comes and watches me play volleyball and drives me home from practice sometimes. We talk a lot about being raised by single mothers." I looked down at my hands, counting the reasons he was special. I struggled to find more examples.

"I'm just asking because I want you to ask yourself if he is worth it. You're the prize, Nina, always remember that. Let Dylan earn your time and energy. Don't give it away for free."

"We are just high school kids. What else can he do? He's not a rich kid like the typical kids in school."

"Nina, I'm not saying that he has to do anything, I'm simply saying to you that you are an extremely beautiful young lady coming into your own and that you are a treasure. Please make these dudes earn the right to have access to your time, energy, and body. Don't sell yourself short or feel obligated to do anything you do not want to do. Not now, not ever."

The words coming from her meant so much. I thought Bryce was one of the most beautiful women that I had ever seen other than my mom. I studied her face and noticed that her milk chocolate skin was flawless, and she always dressed impeccably. Bryce had medium sized breasts and a tiny waist but a large round bottom. I, on the other hand, was shaped like a boy. I was tall, lean, and toned but not curvy. I felt like life was easy for someone like her; she had pretty girl privilege.

"What do you want to do when you finish high school? What are some of your goals?"

Bryce's question made me realize that I never thought about that.

"I'm not sure." I was being honest.

"Well, let me ask you this, do you want to go to college?"

"Yes."

"Okay, well, that's a start. So, now you have a goal. Your goal is to get good grades so that you can get into a great school. Do you have any idea what school you would like to attend? Do you know what you would like to do as an adult?"

"It may sound weird, but I want to go away out of state. I would love to get as far away from my dad and stepmother as possible!"

"Whoa! Really? Is it that bad at home?"

"It's bad. I feel like an outsider. I am not as close to my dad as I was to my mom and my stepmom doesn't want me there."

That was the first time I told someone what I felt my stepmom thought about me. It felt like a weight had lifted off my shoulders. I felt light and airy like I could fly after saying that. It was the elephant in the room between us. She would never say it, but her actions told me all the time that she didn't want me there.

"What has she done to make you feel that way Nina? Is she abusive? Does she hit you?" There was a pause after she asked that question. She placed her hand on my knee and rubbed. She turned to face me.

"I will not share what you say to me in this car. I promise you that you can tell me whatever is on your mind right now. I don't want you making choices and using destructive behavior as a coping method, Nina. It's okay to talk to someone about how you're feeling, and you have the right to feel the way that you do."

"Okay, I just feel like I ruin the perception of my stepmom's perfect family and I also feel like my stepmom has a problem with me trying to be close to my dad."

"What makes you think that? Do you think she's jealous of you? It's not like you his girlfriend, you're his daughter."

"I am not sure if she is jealous of me, but I am sure that I am an unwelcome reminder of the relationship that my dad had with my mother."

"Ah." Bryce was looking up at the roof of her car with her arms crossed as if she was having an *ah ha* moment.

"Do you think there was overlap between him dating your mom and him dating your stepmom?"

"That's the million-dollar question. I'm unsure. At first, I thought it was because Riley, who I was introduced to as my half-sister, and I are not even a full year apart. But then Riley confided in me that my dad was not her dad and that her mom was pregnant when they met. It's all very hush hush and no one dares talk about it. I think my stepmom likes to give the illusion that she and my dad were each other's first love and created and built his business and family from day one together."

"Have you talked to your dad about how you feel?"

"No. That's another thing. With Nicole around, you can't get to my dad within a ten-foot pole. He works long hours already and when he is home, she is on him like a correctional officer to an inmate." Bryce busted out laughing. It was a great way to lighten the mood. My insides were getting warm, and my heart was palpitating, so I knew I was getting upset. "It's like she scared I am going to tell him something that she's not privy too."

"Nina, you are funny to me. I know this is serious, and we will definitely talk more, but that last jab you took at your stepmom, that was priceless. Let's talk more over some ice cream. My greedy ass needs a snack."

My stomach fluttered when we walked into the ice cream shop. The small space was bright with pastel dots all over the floor. The vintage drawings on the wall gave me an Andy Warhol vibe and the high, wooden tables and round chrome bar stools with pastel colored stool covers made me feel like I stepped into an era that was before my time. Bryce and I wrote what type of ice cream we wanted on the notepads.

"What are you getting? It's my treat," Bryce stated.

"Have you been here before?"

"No, not this one. I have never seen this many choices in my life for ice cream sheesh! I want everything." I held the paper up, but had no idea where to start circling.

"You know something, I will just have two scoops of vanilla with rainbow sprinkles."

"You sure, kiddo? You can take your time, no rush."

"I'm sure. What are you getting?"

"I'm getting two scoops of rainbow sherbet with wet

walnuts and crushed pineapples."

I wrinkled my nose but before I said anything Bryce spoke again.

"I know it sounds like a weird hotchpotch combo but it's pretty good together"

"It sounds like a tummy ache" I was rubbing my belly just thinking about her order.

We placed our order then sat down.

"Hey, Nina," a middle-aged, white woman called out to me. She had two small boys who were about eight. The boys ran straight to the front counter, grabbing sheets and a pencil to write down their ice cream orders.

"Hello, ma'am," I said cautiously, not knowing who she was.

"I'm Harper's mom. You guys play on the same volleyball team together." My face relaxed and I smiled.

"Oh okay, Harper is our middle blocker"

"Yes, that's her. I just wanted to tell you that I ran into your mom at the nail salon a couple of days ago. I told her that you were one of the best players I'd seen in a very long time. You're phenomenal at the net, young lady. I asked her if you played club and she told me no."

"Thank you. Nicole's my stepmom, and no I don't play club, but I would love to."

"Really? Because I told your mom to call me if you were interested in playing club. I assumed you weren't interested since we haven't heard anything from you guys. My husband and I own a club called, Dynamic Illusions, and we would love for you to be a part of the Dynamic volleyball family."

I looked at her dumbfounded and speechless. One, she irritated me by calling Nicole my mom after I just corrected her and two because Nicole hadn't mentioned any of this to me. I guess this was my punishment for getting caught having sex with my boyfriend.

"Hello, I'm Bryce; Nina's auntie. Can you tell us a little bit about your club? Is there a website we can visit? What's the cost and time commitment?"

I felt relief when Bryce jumped in and saved me from looking like a complete fool I exhaled. Nicole never mentioned this to me unless she talked it over with my dad and he said no.

"There is a cost and its extensive travel. We practice three times a week for two hours each practice and we play some of the best teams from all over the country. Most of our girls get scholarship offers to play volleyball in college. I'm surprised with your skill level that you aren't already playing club, Nina. Who do you train with?"

"No one other than my high school coach."

"Wow, that's hard to believe. Just imagine how much better you would be if you played all year round. Nina, you would be extremely sought after by D1 schools." Harper's mom saying this made me excited.

"We are definitely going to check your website out. Does

your club offer scholarships?" Damn! Bryce was asking all the right questions.

"Yes, we do. There is an application for scholarships, and we do look at transcripts to make sure the grades are there. We try to save our scholarships for girls who want to play, have the skill level, get good grades, and who can't afford it. It can be an expensive sport."

"Thank you so much. We are going to give this some thought and if we think it is something that we want to explore, we will fill out the scholarship application to see if Nina qualifies. That will be a huge factor before we make a decision."

Bryce was speaking as if she was my mom. It pissed me off when people did that because it made me feel like they were trying to replace my mother, but in this moment, I felt proud having her support. I felt protected and not alone in this world. It was the first time I felt this way since my mother and Ms. Alba had been taken away from me.

"Well, I'm going to be perfectly honest with you ladies and please don't repeat this. I really want Nina to be a part of our club. Nina, you would be a huge asset in helping us get some championship titles under our belt this season. Now, since I sleep with the owner, it is safe for me to say this scholarship will be yours. Of course, you must fill out the paperwork for formalities but if you have the grades and parental consent, we will provide you with the funding."

"I definitely have the grades. I make the honor roll every

semester," I said proudly. My faith wavered when she said parental consent, especially if Nicole had anything to do with it.

"It's mine!" a childlike voice yelled.

"No, it's mine, give it back to me! I had it first!" another child yelled.

"Oh, dear, let me go. My boys are fighting again. Take my card and make sure you remember what I said and call me this time. Nina, we want you on our team!"

"Her hands are full." Bryce laughed with a raised eyebrow, turning her attention to her ice cream the waiter brought over.

"I agree."

"So, what do you make of what she told us?" Bryce asked with a mouth full of ice cream.

"I would love to play for her team but when she said parental consent my hopes left the building."

"You know something, when she said she ran into your stepmom and inquired but Nicole hasn't mentioned anything to you, I immediately understood what you meant earlier in our conversation."

"You do?" It surprised me there was someone in this world who wasn't fooled by Nicole's bullshit.

"Absolutely, why are you sitting there acting shocked? Did you think I didn't believe you?"

"No, it's just everyone loves Nicole and think she is this awesome person that throws fantastic parties and is this perfect wife and mom."

176

"That's because the average person is full of shit. They are impressed with Nicole because of the diamonds and pearls. The big, beautiful home, the fancy car, her label driven attire, and her beauty. Thank goodness I'm not average and I don't care about any of those things." I relaxed my posture and released a sigh of relief.

"I don't know your stepmom personally, but from the very few times I've seen her I can tell what type of person she is. The way she walks into the community center like she owns it, the way she talks down to your grandparents' staff, the way that she deals with that poor nanny."

"Maria, yeah Maria catches hell. They must pay her a fortune because I would've quit. Maria is not a nanny. Maria is a modern-day slave. She does everything in that house." I paused after adding my two cents.

"It just appears like she's not a nice person. She has walked by me on several occasions and looked me dead in my face and didn't speak. I guess she feels that I'm not worthy. I run into people like her all the time, and I see right through them. I bet you she is one of the most insecure women you could ever meet."

"Yikes, Bryce, I didn't think of it this way. I don't know why she would be insecure."

"We always talk about Nicole but what's up with your dad, Nina? Let's talk about him some. Are you scared to reach out to him? I mean, you have a driver, and you have me. Why haven't you dropped into his office? Bring him lunch? Force a dialogue?" I blinked, trying to hold back tears. Bryce looked perplexed.

"What's wrong, Nina? Why are you getting upset? I can see it in your face. What are you not telling me?" Bryce looked concerned.

"Honestly?" I asked weakly.

"Honestly," Bryce repeated, grabbing my hand, and rubbing it gently.

I felt extremely vulnerable. I looked around at the hustle and bustle around us and felt Bryce rub my arm.

"Let's go sit outside on the bench near the grass area." I grabbed my sweet treat and followed Bryce.

"I wanted to give you all my attention and I want you to take your time and breath, Nina. Tell me what's going on. Why are you scared of your dad?"

I took a deep breath and tears filled my eyes.

"It's okay, Nina. You can cry. We are emotional creatures and crying is okay."

"Rejection," I whispered so low I could barely hear myself. Bryce was quiet and stared at me quietly, waiting for me to finish.

"Bryce, he already shown me that he chose his life here over me and my mom. He decided that I wasn't worth the fight and left me home while he and his family vacationed. Every time I think I want to find out why... I get nervous about his truth and what he may tell me. At this point, I have no one else, so getting scraps of whatever attention or parenting Santino gives me is better than the alternative. I'm in the eleventh grade and I'm just biding my time. If I'm being honest, it's easier to be mad with Nicole instead of my dad, I can attribute her meanness to her not being my blood but my father's truth, knowing his real truth may not be something that I can handle right now. So, no, I don't want to push him, and I don't want to force myself. I want him to naturally want to spend time with me and when I feel the time is right, like I can handle what he has to say then I'll push harder."

"Nina, I heard what you said, and I respect that decision if that is how you feel. Just let me know how I can best support you. I want you to soar and live your best life. You deserve that and that means doing whatever it is that makes you happy. If that's playing travel ball to avoid having one of the toughest talks of your life, then that's what we will do. But I do believe you owe it to yourself to get answers from your dad. I guess you just have to do it in your own time because you have to be prepared to be able to receive what he responds back to you. I think your dad loves you, it's just in a different way that you are used to being loved. I won't push it any further. In the meantime, let's see about getting you to play for this volleyball club."

"I believe and agree with everything you just said but getting her and my dad's consent will most likely not happen. They can afford it, but Nicole will find a way to make this not happen. My dad is aloof, and I have completely lost faith in his ability to parent me. If you can allow your wife to leave your daughter out of a family vacation, then you are a shitty human. But I digress," I said, laughing, which was the first time I found something to laugh about, and it felt good.

"Well, doll, to play devil's advocate there is power in the punani. I am about a decade older than you and I know this to be a fact. Don't worry about the consent part. I think I may have a plan."

"Really what? You're gonna seduce my dad?"

"Ewwww, hell no! Damn, Nina, is that what you think of me?" Bryce was holding her spoon in the air.

"Your daddy is fine but a little too old for me. Plus, what I won't do is mess with a married man. I'm way too good for that, and I deserve and demand a man of my own. I don't share. Now, if he has any fine ass single younger brothers then maybe I can be your auntie for real."

"Girl bye! He has three but they just as screwed up as he is."

I laughed out loud, and the people walking by were looking at us and smiling. I revisited our conversation while we walked to the car.

"Bryce, what is your plan to get my parents to consent?" I was eager to know because I realized volleyball was one of the very few things that brought me joy. If I could play longer than my high school season that would be fantastic.

"Your Greats. What I noticed about Nicole when she walks her stuck-up ass into the center and saunters past me like I am invisible is that she seeks approval from your grandparents and great grandparents. If we can get them on board before going to your parents, it may help us. I just don't see her going against what they say."

"Bingo, that's brilliant and I think you are right because there is something fishy about my Grandma Sabrina and my stepmom. I don't think my grandma is fond of her. I've seen her shut her down several times."

"Good. How's your relationship with your grandparents? I don't know them too well. I've only seen them in the center once or twice."

"Well, it's weird because to me, my grandma is an older version of Nicole, just nicer. I get along with them very well, but they travel a lot and do their thing. I don't spend as much time with them as I do my Greats."

"Okay, well, let's get going. I think we need to make a visit to your great-grandparents' home."

"Let's do it." I felt more optimistic and stoked.

Chapter Twenty-one

"Umm, Grandma Diane, this smells amazing." The smell of cinnamon and vanilla filled the air. My grandma and I baking together have become one of my favorite pastimes.

"You see, now all of that peeling and dicing apples was worth it. Sometimes you have to put in the time and effort to be able to enjoy the reward. Wait until we dig into this pie, your grandpa made his fresh homemade ice cream to go on top so this will be a glorious treat."

Ding Dong

"Go get the door, dear. It's probably your dad."

"Sure, Grandma." I walked to the door nervously. My Greats were going to speak to my dad about me playing travel ball and I wasn't sure of the outcome.

"Hey Dad! Hey Nicole," I said nonchalantly, letting them inside. My dad hugged me a little longer than I expected.

"What's been going on, baby girl. Seems like I haven't gotten a chance to see you in forever. You've been spending more time with Granny than with me." My dad was so full of shit. I plastered a fake smile and played the game. If he wanted to be full of shit, then I would be full of shit with him.

"You've been working so much lately. I honestly thought you moved out of the family home and was now living in your office building."

"Ha ha! Someone has jokes today. I do what I have to do to take care of all of my beautiful women."

"And Greyson," Nicole added. "We can't forget our prince."

"Greyson is the least demanding in the house. My son is easy." My dad laughed.

I wasn't sure what he meant by that because I didn't ask him for shit. I would rather do without.

"Grandma D, what's that smelling so good up in here?" my dad yelled, walking toward the kitchen. I felt Nicole's eyes on me when I closed the door.

"Have a seat, dear. Why are you standing like a statue in the middle of the floor?" my grandpa asked Nicole. My grandpa was a military retiree and always direct.

"Of course, Grandpa Mario. I guess I was waiting for Nina

to offer me a seat."

"Why? Nina don't live here, and you have been here a thousand times. What you just said don't make no sense."

I laughed on the inside. I was always happy when someone checked Nicole on her foolishness.

My dad walked back into the living room with a large slice of apple pie and a glob of ice cream then plopped down on the couch near my grandpa.

"It's a shame that we have to bribe you to come over with homemade apple pie and fresh ice cream. That don't make no sense, Tino." My grandpa hiked his pant legs up, revealing his black nylon socks.

"Pops, you don't have to bribe me. I love coming over here. You guys know I stay busy with the business."

"Bullshit, son. You make time for what you want to make time for. I'm old but I ain't crazy."

"Pops, you know that I love you and I love spending time with you, but I barely spend time with my own family. You know I got a million kids," my dad joked, leaning back into my grandma, who was now sitting on the opposite side of him, kissing her cheek.

"Mema, you know I love you to pieces, right?" he asked my grandma.

"Yes, I know." She patted his leg and leaned her face in to accept all the sugar he was giving her.

"Well, grandson, at least Nina spends time with us. We

have grown to love her so much and I wish we spent more time with her when she was younger," my grandpa said in a regretful tone.

"Let's not talk about the past, Grandpa Mario. I am here now and you're still young and we still have a lot of time together," I said, hugging him.

"You're so sweet. Did you eat some pie, baby?"

"You know I did. I got it when it first came out the oven. It's so good, Grandma."

"You helped me during the whole process this time so you should be able to make it now on your own."

"Baby girl, if you can make this for your daddy, I would be forever grateful. This is my absolute favorite pie," my dad said, inhaling his dessert.

"Really?" I squealed. "Daddy, homemade apple pie is my absolute favorite pie also. My mom used to bake it for me when I got good grades, my birthday, and all of the holidays. I love apple pie." I was excited to have something in common with my dad. It made me giddy like a little kid.

"Honey, it's almost four and we have to meet the Barringer's at six for dinner." Nicole always knew how to ruin the mood.

"Well, since Nicole has made it apparent that our time is limited, I guess we will get to the point," my grandpa said, irritated.

"Pops, your time is never limited. We have plenty of time.

What's up?"

"Why can't Nina play volleyball?" my grandpa blurted out. He leaned on the edge of his chair with his hand on his knee. He leaned closer to my dad and moved his glasses down to look over them. I guess adjusting his glasses would make him hear the response better.

"Pops, what are you talking about. Nina does play volleyball. You've watched her play. She is a starting player on her high school varsity team."

"No, son. We are talking about the woman who is interested in her playing travel volleyball where she can possibly play in college and get scholarships. If it's too expensive then we can help pay for it."

"I'm not sure what woman you're talking about. I can afford for her to play travel ball. I had no idea she was interested. Why didn't you just ask me, Nina?" The look on my dad's face let me know he was clueless.

"I had no idea neither, Daddy. Harper, who plays on my team, mom approached me in the ice cream shop last week and said she spoke with Nicole about me joining the Dynamic Illusion volleyball team. Her and her husband own the travel team and she told me that I would be a great addition to help them win a championship game. She also told me she had been waiting for us to call her back and let her know but hadn't heard anything."

My dad looked across the living room at Nicole, who sat frozen with her legs crossed and hands extended on the arms of the chair.

"Oh yeah. She approached me at the girls' game," Nicole said.

"Well, why didn't you say something to me?" my dad questioned, sitting his plate down on the end of the table.

She has watched me play. I don't remember seeing Nicole at a volleyball game, I thought.

"Well, honey, I didn't think you would want our daughter playing volleyball all over the country without supervision. You would never be able to attend because you spend the majority of your time working and they travel extensively. I wouldn't be able to go because of the three kids that we have at the house."

I wondered if she heard what she was saying. Ryan and Riley were close in age as me and Maria raised Greyson, so who was she kidding right now.

"Nicole, you still should have discussed this with me," my dad said.

Wow, he may just have a backbone, I thought.

"Nicole, I just don't understand why you wouldn't pursue an opportunity like this for Nina." My grandpa took off his wire, circular rimmed glasses and used them to point at Nicole.

"Well, the fact that she wouldn't have a chaperone is what concerns me—"

My dad cut her off.

"Nicole, I still do not understand why you didn't talk to me about it, and before you say it's because I work long hours, let's remember that just this week you manage to speak to me about getting Riley a new car, getting Greyson tennis lessons, and sending you on a girls' trip to LA next month to enjoy a self-care weekend." He smoothed his jeans and sat at the edge of the couch. He added a little bass in his voice and stared at Nicole. I jumped in, trying to break up the tension.

"The team travels together in a private motor coach. We also fly together if it's a place that's too far to drive. We all stay in the same hotel. When we spoke with Harper's mom, she said most players' parents do not travel with the team to the tournaments because of the extensive travel schedule."

"Nina, what's the cost?" my dad asked, looking directly at Nicole.

"It's twelve thousand a year but they have scholarships that they give if you have good grades to help offset cost."

"You can go," my dad said.

"They also have payment plans so that you do not have to pay all at one time… huh?"

Did I hear my dad correctly? Is he talking to me or telling Nicole I could go? They stared each other down like they were about to face-off.

"You heard me, baby girl. You can join the team." I jumped up and down. I hugged my dad and ran to the couch to hug my Greats. Bryce hit this one on the head. I needed to call her and let her know the good news.

"You sure about that husband, dear." Nicole gave him a

cold stare.

"Why wouldn't I be sure, Nicole?" my dad challenged.

"Oh, and Nina forget the scholarship application. Let a child in need apply for that and utilize those funds. *I* can afford it," my dad emphasized. I wasn't sure if he was throwing a dig at his wife who hadn't worked since they married.

Nicole then scooted closer to the edge of her seat, intensifying her stare at my dad. She glared at me then back at my dad. I suddenly got a bad feeling in the pit of my stomach. My lungs felt like I was losing air. I tried to breathe but my body was in a state of paralysis with air trapped in my lungs, bile in my throat, and butterflies in my stomach. This was the very first time that I prayed for God to take away Nicole's breath...

Chapter Twenty-Two

"Sooo, Nina, having sex with random boys wouldn't bother you?" Nicole scoffed, freezing me in place. There it was. Confirmation that she was the ultimate bitch. My grandma gasped and threw daggers at Nicole. I sat quietly and exhaled. A pain riddled through my body, and I felt a warm sensation on my face like someone slapped me. It was something about the way a maternal figure who was not my mom, but a mom, displayed glee at exposing something so deeply shameful and personal about a child; not her child, but her husband's child that pierced my already fractured heart. Nicole's callous behavior showed me no mercy; she was out for blood.

"That's a hateful thing to say, Nicole." My grandma's chest was rising and falling. I could tell Nicole's welcome was worn out at this point.

"Why would you say some shit like that about my child, Nicole?" My dad stood.

"I *would* say it because it's true. Nancy Umstead, Dylan's mom, called me and told me that she caught Nina having sex with Dylan in her home a couple of weeks ago. I didn't tell you because I didn't want to upset you. But since you don't want me holding anything back from you, I guess I made a grave mistake in not telling you."

I dropped my phone and looked at my dad. He was staring at me. I couldn't look at my Greats because I couldn't bear to see their faces. My mouth was open, and I was speechless.

"Nina, why don't you tell your dad. Come on, baby girl. Let him know that you were sneaking into Dylan's house while his poor mother worked to earn money for their household. Imagine her surprise when she came home early to see you in a compromising position with her son."

"Is this true, Nina?" My dad looked at me with pleading eyes as if he wanted me to say it was not true. I didn't say anything at all. I snatched my phone and ran out of the front door, bursting into tears. I never felt more embarrassed and ashamed in my entire life.

"Hurry up, Nina, before somebody comes in here." Dylan

was impatient and nervous. When my dad found out we had sex, I was grounded without my phone. We resorted to having sex at my school before games. Dylan was permitted on campus as a spectator, and he wore a version of our school's uniform. I was in a dangerous mindset of completely not giving a fuck and my behavior was becoming reckless.

My dad punished me. He only allowed me to go to school, play volleyball, and come home. I wasn't permitted to go to the community center or to my great grandparents' house for a month. This was a joke to me; my father had no time for me and didn't do a thing parental outside of provide but handed down a punishment like he earned that right. My mother would've spoken to me about my actions, asked me what made me do whatever it was that I did. She would tell me that although she was disappointed that she still loved me unconditionally. She would punish me and explain that my actions had consequences but as a parent, everything Omalara did to and for Santina was out of love. The love from a parent to a child who understood that mistakes were a part of learning and growing. My mother believed a huge part of parenting was course correcting your children and realigning them toward a better pathway.

Santino did none of that and as a result, I was slowly perishing on the inside. I was too ashamed to face my Greats so stolen moments with Dylan had been my only solace. I'd risk any punishment that was handed down to feel a few minutes of bliss.

"I'm trying but you got on these stupid khakis with buttons

instead of a zipper like normal pants." I pulled Dylan's bottoms down and got on my knees to give him a blow job.

"Ummm, wow, BK... yes... baby... go faster."

"Shut up before you get us in trouble." I released his penis long enough to warn him to shut up. I put my head back down, taking in his manhood until it hit the back of my throat. I gripped his waist with my hands and bobbed back and forth until I felt his penis pulsating in my mouth, indicating a climax.

"Aaaahhhhhh, shit." Dylan fell back onto the locker and closed his eyes like he was about to take a quick nap.

"Fix your clothes," I whispered, tapping him on his chest. "We are in school, which means you don't have time to bask in the glory of your orgasm. Hurry up and get out before my team comes in here to change for the game."

"Alright. Good luck, bae." Dylan bit my neck, slapped my ass, and slid out of the locker room.

"Thanks." I ran to the back of the locker room to get my baby wipes.

"Nina, Nina! Are you in here?"

"Riley?" I whispered. I threw my headphones in quickly, wiped my face, and stayed quiet. I prayed she thought the locker room was empty and left. I also hoped she didn't see Dylan leaving the locker room.

"There you are! Guess what?" Riley was excited as she pulled off my headphones. I looked up from tying my shoes.

"Hey, Riley. What's up?"

"I'm playing with you today!"

"What do you mean?"

"Coach pulled me up from junior varsity to varsity! We get to play together on the same team!"

"Wow! That's great, Riley! When did this happen?"

"Just now! Coach King and Coach Hoot pulled me to the side and told me I wouldn't play with my team today. When I asked why, Coach King said because he wanted me to play on varsity. They have seen some vast improvements and felt like I would be a great asset to your team."

"As an outside hitter?" I questioned. I didn't want to sound like I wasn't excited, but I was an outside hitter and Riley was weak at this position. The situation baffled me. She was in no way an asset to varsity.

"Yep. Isn't this fantastic! Two sisters playing the same position and dominating the team."

"Yes. This is going to be a great season," I said dryly.

As the other players filled the locker room, my mind was going in several directions.

"Hey, Nina, you ready to show August Martin High School what we got? Showtime is in less than thirty." Harper walked right by Riley and gave me a high five.

"I am more than ready."

"Hey, Harper. I'm playing on varsity now with you guys," Riley chimed in proudly.

"Yeah, whatever," Harper said and walked away. Riley looked at me and I hunched my shoulders.

"You ready, sis? Let's go. It's game time." I pumped my fist in the air while using my other hand to pat Riley on the back. We made our way into the gym.

I walked into the gym and noticed Nicole. It was strange because I never saw her attend a game— not one of mine anyway. I guessed since Riley was on the team, she felt we were worthy of her attendance.

I scanned the crowd and saw her talking to Addison's mom. I hated Addison. I didn't hate her because she was my competition on the team, but she displayed a type of privilege on the court no one else could. She was rude to the coaches. If she had a bad game, she showed poor sportsmanship, and she talked back to the refs if she didn't agree with their calls. Addison was the worst type of player and no one on the team liked her. We tolerated her because she was a decent player, but her attitude was horrible.

"Nina, we're going to start Riley!" Coach yelled when I was making my way to the court.

What the fuck, I thought to myself.

"Okay." I sat down on the bench and stared into space. I wasn't sure how in the hell all of this was happening.

Buzzzz

August Martin served the ball. Kelsey, our server, passed the ball to Hannah. Hannah set the ball to Riley.

Smack

Riley tried to kill the ball but didn't jump off the ground and it landed in the net. We lost the first point.

"That's okay, baby. Keep swinging!" Nicole yelled.

I rested my chin on my fists, watching from the sidelines.

Smack

August Martin served the ball directly at Riley. Riley shanked the ball into the crowd. I closed my eyes tightly. I wondered how many girls on the team knew she was my sister. I prayed no one did.

August Martin served again. They served it directly to Riley again and Kelsey stepped in front of Riley, delivering a perfect pass to our setter. This time, the setter set Harper and Harper slapped the ball down, giving us our first point.

"Harrrrr-ppperrrrr!" I stood up, clapping. "Let's keep it going team." I stood up and watched the next play. It was our turn to serve.

August Martin received the ball, set it, and their outside hitter smacked the ball hard. It came across the net high, going out of the court.

"I got it!" Riley yelled. The ball was way out of bounds, but since Riley touched it, they got the point.

Why did her stupid ass touch a ball that was out! I screamed in my head.

Coach King slammed the clipboard against his forehead.

"Nina! You're going in for Riley next rotation." I looked at him and I nodded.

The fuck you take me out for anyway when I get the majority of the teams kills, I thought to myself. This had to be Nicole's doing. I checked the scoreboard before jumping into the game.

Shit

We were down by six just that fast. I knew I needed to block everything out and focus because every play counted. I bent my knees low, getting in position to receive August Martin's serve.

Smack

I delivered the perfect pass before running to the sidelines so Hannah could set the ball to me. I jumped up like I had springs in my sneakers and hit the ball with fire.

August Martin wasn't ready when the ball flew over the net. It went through the blocker's hands and landed right in an empty hole I aimed for on my opponent's side.

"In!" the flag girl yelled.

My team yelled and jumped up and down. Coach King pumped his fist to his raised knee. During our quick huddle, my team told me I did a great job.

"Let's get back on top one point at a time." I got back into the ready position, waited for my teammate to serve, then glanced at the stands. Nicole looked stiff and constipated. I would show her that although she ruled our home, I dominated this court.

After we garnered the final point, the final buzzer rang. August Martin were tough opponents, but we managed to win.

"Great game, girls. You guys had me nervous for a moment." I looked at the coach like he was a unicorn. His lineup is what had the team screwed.

"Everybody give it up for Nina. She is our MVP tonight!"

"Nina! Nina!" A couple of the girls chanted while I smiled, doing a victory dance.

"Coach! Nina was the MVP? I got like fifteen kills today." I could tell Addison was pissed.

"You got eighteen kills today, Addison," the coach said in a matter-of-fact tone while holding up the stats.

"However, Nina got twenty-nine kills, and eleven aces, which makes her MVP." The coach stared her down. She turned her red face toward her knee pads, pulling them down.

"Nina for the win!" my teammate, Kelsey, yelled.

"Thank you, guys, it was definitely a team effort. We still have two more games before we get to the championship so let's keep pushing," All the girls cheered, putting our fists up in a circle yelling. "One. Two. Three. Wildcats!"

Addison wasn't in the huddle. She was making her way toward the locker rooms.

"Bitch," Harper said, looking in her direction. I ignored Harper's comment and laughed. One thing my mother taught me was to never engage or acknowledge gossip because high school girls were all two faced.

I sat quietly with my headphones in during the ride home. Nicole and Riley replayed the game and Nicole told her she was proud. I listened. I wasn't playing any music and curious about their conversation. Nicole was delusional. Riley played for a few minutes in one set and caused us to lose several points back-to-back, so I wasn't sure what game Nicole watched.

"Mom, I don't think the girls on varsity like me. Can you talk to the coach about that?"

"I can do one better; I'll throw a little gathering at the house for the team. We can call it a team bonding event. Addison's mom and I spoke about it today."

"That's a horrible idea because everyone hates Addison too!" Riley screamed.

"Calm down, Riley, and let me handle it. It's just because Addison is their star player and she's a little cocky and you're new. The girls will come around," Nicole assured her.

"I'm not sure about that. Nina is our star player, Mom. Did you not pay attention to the game tonight?"

I bopped my head to non-existent music; I didn't say a word and continued looking out the window.

"Nina lives in the house with us so if I throw a party and they are fond of her, they will come."

"Yeah, that's true. Except Addison. She hates Nina because

they play the same position and Nina is better than her. I doubt she will come."

"She will. I already spoke to her mom."

"Okay, Ma, if you say so." Riley put on headphones as well.

"Riley, before you get lost in that music, last question. Was that guy in the jean jacket Nina's boyfriend, Dylan?" I perked up because Nicole was being nosey.

"Yeah. Why?" Riley quizzed.

"Well, I saw him cheering for her and yelling her name. I was curious."

"Oh yeah, that's him," Riley responded, placing her headphones back on her head.

The rest of the ride was quiet. Once we entered the house, I grabbed some grapes and went straight to my room. I took a long, warm shower and went into my closet. I teared up, looking at my mother's mural. It was beautiful. I missed her so much. It took me almost a year, but I was happy with the details and intricacies I drew in her face, hair, and collarbone. The punishment handed down from my father for having sex with Dylan gave me the seclusion and focus I needed to complete the mural. I talked to her for the next thirty minutes before I laid down and went to sleep.

Chapter Twenty-three

It had been a rough couple of weeks for me personally, but a stellar end to the game season for me as an athlete. I was laser focused and my game showed it. Santino made Nicole wait until the season was over to throw a gathering and allowed me to invite Dylan. The olive branch had been extended but deep down inside I was scared to reach for it. My insecurities of his parenting skills left a wall around my heart that I was not ready to completely remove for him, but Bryce talked me into taking baby steps and try. The used two-tone Toyota Camry helped coax me into trying as well. It wasn't brand new like Riley and Ryan's first cars, but I didn't care. I was grateful for it, and it was a really nice whip.

"Thank you guys for coming to Riley and Nina's gathering." Tino commanded everyone's attention.

"Congratulations on winning the state championship!"

"Yaaay!" everyone cheered.

"Congratulations to my daughter, Nina, for being our high school varsity volleyball team's most valuable player!"

Everyone went wild in the basement when my dad said that. Dylan squeezed my hand and lifted it in the air. I smiled wide and proud. Not because I was the MVP, but because my dad said my name proudly. It had been a rough year. I was surprised he knew I did well this season.

"Now, I want everyone to have a great time. The bathroom is in the back corner. We have plenty of food and drinks. The DJ will play whatever it is you kids like to listen to nowadays...the clean version of course. Mingle and have fun. You guys deserve this. You worked hard this season. Now turn up!" Ryan, Riley, and I placed our hands on our heads.

"Dad, you were doing so good until that last line!" I yelled out at him.

"What? That's not what you guys say?" Everyone laughed and the DJ started the music. I let go of Dylan's hand and walked over to my dad. I hugged his waist, pressing the side of my face into his chest.

"Thanks, Dad, for shouting me out and thanks for the party. Everything looks amazing."

He pulled me away from his chest and placed his hands on

my shoulders. He looked proud.

"You're welcome, kiddo. You know we haven't always seen eye to eye but overall, I am super proud of you, Nina. You have blown us away with your grades. You have colleges interested in you for their volleyball programs. I can't believe you will be a senior soon and leaving us for college. I feel like we just got you."

"You feel like I just moved in here, Daddy? I feel like I've been living here for a hundred years already!" I added my weird humor to his emotional words as a ploy not to cry. I longed to hear those words and wished his actions backed them up a lot more, but I would take what I could get.

"Oh, you got jokes, baby girl?" he said, laughing and pinching my nose gently.

"Dad, do you think you can behave long enough for me to introduce you to my boyfriend?"

"Nah, let that little nigga stay his ass in the corner away from me." My dad's face went from warm to stern. He crossed his arms across his chest and looked directly at Dylan.

"Daddy, don't be like that. I really like him, and he's scared of you...stop staring him down like that."

"Like what?" My dad was talking to me but glared at Dylan.

"What's up, fam. Who we mean mugging?" I felt an arm on my shoulder. When I looked up, my Uncle Legend was looking at Dylan.

"This little asswipe in the corner. Nina's little friend."

"Oh, that's him? That's that cat Dylan. Let me go introduce myself," my uncle said.

"Good idea, little brother. Let's do that." My dad snapped out of his gaze and started walking. My stomach dropped. My dad and uncle looked like giants walking over to Dylan.

"Yo, who are you? You go to Nina's school?" my uncle snapped.

"Huh… yeah, I mean no… I go… to to…" Dylan stuttered while looking up at my uncle.

"That shit don't matter, I don't care where you go. How do you know my niece?"

My Uncle Legend was being rude. He cut him off and that intimidated Dylan. It made Dylan's voice leave him. He looked like a deer caught in headlights.

"He's just joking with you, Dylan. This is my Uncle Legend, my dad's baby brother, and this is my dad, Tino. They both are excited to meet you." My voice was shaky. Wringing my hands, a nervous chuckle escaped my mouth, and my stomach was doing flips.

"No, I'm not!" my uncle yelled out.

"No, you not my uncle?" I questioned in disbelief.

"Stop tripping, Nina. Of course, I'm your favorite uncle, but no I'm not excited to meet his ass," my uncle said, jabbing his thumb toward Dylan.

"Oh, and my name is not Tino," my dad added.

"What? Daddy, if your name is not Tino then what is it?" They were irritating me.

"My name is Mr. Wellington."

"Daddy...why so formal? Stop being mean!" my voice pleaded with him.

"Nah, we all the way formal. As a matter of fact, call me Mr. Wellington too," my Uncle Legend chimed in.

"Nice to meet you both." Dylan extended his hand toward my uncle. Uncle Legend put his hands in his pockets, turned around, and walked away. When my dad grabbed his hand to shake it, his massive hand enveloped Dylan's. Dylan winced as my dad stared at him.

"Okay, Daddy, thank you for being so kind and meeting my boyfriend," I said, trying to pry my dad's grip loose one finger at a time.

Shit, my dad is stronger than a motherfucker.

"Enjoy the party and have fun." He broke his grip finally and snapped out of his glare. My dad pulled me close and kissed my forehead, I was shaking in my dress.

"Have fun, baby girl. I'm watching your ass, Dylan." He rolled his eyes hard at Dylan, walked off, and mingled with some of the parents who stayed to help chaperone the party.

"Damn, that was intense." Dylan took a deep breath and bent over with his hands on his knees.

"Sorry. Damn, I didn't know they would act like that. I had no idea my uncle would be here. Let's just pray the others don't show up. Uncle Legend is the least crazy of the bunch," I said, rubbing his back.

Nicole was walking toward us, but I pretended not to see her.

"Let's go to the drink table." I heard Nicole call my name as we walked away. The music was loud, so I pretended not to hear her. Unfortunately, she caught up with us at the drink table.

"Hey guys, I was calling you."

"Oh, hey, Nicole," I said in an unwelcoming tone.

"Hey, Mrs. Wellington," Dylan said leery. I guess he wasn't sure what to expect after what my dad and uncle did to him. Honestly, I never knew what to expect from Nicole.

"You can call me Nicole," she purred, extending her hand. Dylan looked at her hand and lifted his hand slowly to shake hers. He looked around like it was a trap.

"I saw that you met my husband and was jealous that I'm the last one to meet you. Nina, are you embarrassed by me?" She placed her hands on her chest, looking at me sideways.

"Why am I the last one to meet your boyfriend? Your grandparents even told me that they met him already." I didn't have an answer, so I changed the subject.

"Great party, Nicole," I said.

"Yeah, great party," Dylan mimicked.

"We're going to go dance now, talk to you later."

I pulled Dylan by the arm and walked toward the makeshift dance floor where some of my teammates were doing a line dance.

Looking back, I saw Nicole staring at us every time the strobe light hit her face in the dimly lit basement.

"Your stepmom seems nice. But she must have forgotten that I've met her before." I snapped my head toward Dylan, puzzled.

"Where have you met my stepmom before?"

"At the community center. I guess she forgot but she introduced me to Riley a couple of weeks ago. She was there with Addison and her mom. They were using the gym for a private volleyball lesson with Coach King."

"Really? Why didn't you tell me that?" I was pissed. I assumed that's why Coach King started Riley and benched me. I guess his lessons weren't enough because she barely played since being pulled up to varsity.

"I couldn't. You were grounded and didn't have access to your phone and when we were able to sneak in a conversation, your sister was the last person I wanted to talk about." I agreed with him on that and nodded my head.

"I am so glad to be off punishment. I look forward to spending more time with my great- grandparents and my mentee at the community center."

"Who Ashley?"

"Yeah, she's interested in playing volleyball and I made an agreement with her that for every hour we studied math, I would give her thirty minutes of volleyball training. She's in middle school so it's the perfect time to start teaching her some techniques."

I missed Ashley so much. I grew fond of her and was so upset that my dad and Nicole cut me off from tutoring her while I was on punishment. They took away the community center, using Dylan as the reason.

"Well, she may have found another mentor."

"What!" I yelled.

"Riley and Addison have been tutoring her in math and showing her some volleyball tips while you been gone."

This was unbelievable. I swear everything I loved was taken from me in some way, shape, or form. It deepened my hate for Nicole and her fucking offspring.

Chapter Twenty-four

My junior year was ending and the last couple of months went by pretty smoothly. One of the hardest things I had to do was talk with my Greats about my sexual behavior and apologize to them. I don't know why but it felt necessary and what they thought of me mattered. They went into stories about their first time and how young they were. They made sure that I knew that I was still loved and that they weren't judging me at all. My heart was ripped out of my body when my mother was taken away from me, but God knew that I needed someone to love me. When he gave me Mario and Diane Wellington, he gave me greatness. It didn't remove the loss I felt but it helped me remember how amazing it felt to be loved.

I resumed my routine of going to church with my Greats and spending time in the community center. I was now teaching young kids the basics in drawing. I confided in Bryce about my passion and even showed her my mother's mural and she encouraged me to share my gift with others while donating tons of art supplies and easels. My Greats was impressed with my skills and made me promise to make them something, so I committed myself to re-creating their wedding portrait and gifting it to them on their 65th anniversary in a couple of months.

I worked on their portrait in the basement, which gave me an excuse to be down there for hours on end without interruption. They hardly ever came down the steep steps, but this solidified my privacy and made me more careless with sneaking Dylan into the basement. Dylan was going to Fayetteville State University, which wasn't far away but the thought of that one-hour distance made me want to spend as much time with him as possible.

This weekend, I planned to spend time with Dylan to cheer him up because he was disappointed that he didn't get the financial aid he needed to go to his dream school, Morehouse College. The fact that he got accepted but couldn't afford it made the sting so much worse.

Dylan was deep inside of me with his tongue. We laid on top of two, thick blankets I placed on the basement floor. Dylan turned me around and entered me from the back.

"Ummm!" I yelled. Dylan covered my mouth.

"SSSHHHH! I don't want your grandparents to hear us," he whispered, looking around. I grabbed my panties off the floor and stuffed them in my mouth to prevent making noises.

Dylan was going too slow for my taste. My insides were on fire. I placed my hand on the wall and slammed my ass cheeks into Dylan's manhood.

When I looked back at Dylan, his eyes were closed but his hands were gripping the sides of my waist. I felt his fingers pressing deeply into my skin. Dylan was pumping back and forth. In record speed, Dylan collapsed on my back.

"Damn, BK," he whispered, rolling over.

I got up and went into the small half bath where I smuggled a towel and washcloths downstairs. I lathered the washcloth and walked back to where Dylan was laying.

"Ah, girl, that wash cloth is hot." He grabbed his manhood and sat straight up.

"Wrap the condom up and place it in this tissue and take it with you. I don't want to risk flushing it down my grandparents' toilet or putting it in the garbage down here. It would be my luck the toilet back up or someone find it in the trash."

"I know right. Let me put it in my backpack. I'll toss it on my way home." He placed the used condom inside of a paper towel and placed it in his bookbag.

"Speaking of condoms, guess who gave me several packs." Dylan was looking at me perplexed with raised brows.

"Who? The nice lady from the community center that give seminars on safe sex?" I asked.

"Nope, guess again."

I hated guessing games.

"Bryce? She knows we date but I can't imagine her giving you condoms. I damn sure know it wasn't my great-grandparents." Dylan looked at me from the sofa.

"Oh, shit my Greats gave you condoms?" I whispered loudly.

"No, your stepmother did."

"What?" I didn't whisper this time.

"Stop fucking lying, Dylan." I turned around and picked up the blankets.

"I am not lying, Nina. She rolled up on me after school today. I was walking to my car, and she was standing near it. She asked me if we could go to the pizza shop because she wanted to talk to me."

"Yoooo, why are you just telling me this."

"You were in practice, and you know you can't have your phone. Plus, I knew we made arrangements to see each other today so I am telling you now."

"Well, what else did she say?" I moved closer to Dylan with my hands squeezed together in between my knees and paid attention to every word.

"Well, I told her I couldn't go with her to the pizza shop. I didn't trust riding in her car. I felt like it was a set up. I told her I had to go to work. Then she placed her hand on my door, blocking me from opening it, saying she only needed fifteen minutes of my time."

"What the fuck? She forced you to listen to her?"

"Yes. Yoooo, she way too fine to be crazy. She's scary as shit. Where your dad find her at?" I ignored that fine comment and rolled my eyes at him. He was getting on my damn nerves and talking too slow for me.

"I have no idea, Dylan. Maybe he found her in the trash? Maybe on the side of the road! Who knows? What else did she say?"

"She was like I know you're having sex with my daughter and for some reason you seem to be into her, and you better be having safe sex." Dylan was talking in a high pitch tone, trying to mimic a woman's voice.

"Huh? Like she cares anything about me. She has some nerves...she actually referred to me as her daughter?"

"Yep, she said no matter what Nina thinks of me, I love her, and I want the best for her."

"Yeah, fucking right."

"I know. I didn't say a word back to her, but I was thinking after all the hell she put you through. Had me blue balling for almost a damn month. Maaaan, please."

"What did you say?"

"Nothing. I didn't say a damn thing to this lady. I was shocked as hell and couldn't move my mouth to say a word." I believed him. If he was anything like the day my dad and uncle rolled up on him at my party, I knew he was frozen and shocked.

"Then she said if you guys are sneaking around and having

sex, I want you guys to be safe. She then handed me this." He reached into his backpack and pulled out a small black gift bag. He flipped the gift bag upside down and condoms fell out.

"Wow. I wonder if she is supplying Ryan and Riley with condoms. Riley is literally fucking half the basketball team."

"Don't forget Ryan hooked up with Jerrod and that Spanish cat off the football team. I heard she hooked up with him too."

"Damn, I hadn't heard that. I overheard her telling Riley about her boyfriend, Zach, on the basketball team that she had sex in his Range Rover. They stopped talking when I walked in the room, but little do they know I could care less."

"You think Nicole knows about her and Zach?"

"Yep, she knows. She magically is allowed to have him over every so often."

"Oh really. That's weird because she kept asking me if I thought Riley was pretty."

"What?" I was pissed off now.

"Yep, she actually said to me *'don't you think my Riley is pretty...most young guys like light skin girls with curly hair like my girls Riley and Ryan.'*"

"What a lowdown bitch. You know that does not surprise me because she has said some mean things to me before about my hair and my skin color."

"I remember you telling me that. Shit, you fine as fuck like Lauren Hill and Naomi Campbell." His comment made me smile.

"Well, at least she saved us money on condoms." I was

waving one of them in the air.

"Let me see that." Dylan snatched the condom away from me and rubbed his hand across it.

"Nina, this has a small hole in it." I snatched it back to look at it closely.

"Let me see that," I quipped.

"I don't see any holes."

"Rub your hand across it. Come here, let me see something." I held it up to the light and saw two fine pin holes. Dylan grabbed another condom and held it up to the lamp.

"Nina, this one has a hole in it also, look."

"Oh my God! Dylan. Why would she do this? This is fucking insane."

"I am not sure but throw these shits in the garbage. There is no way we are using any of these." Dylan put them back in the bag to toss them.

"Nina, I am not sure what's going on with your stepmother but be careful. She sounds a tad bit crazy."

"A tad bit? She is a whole lot of crazy; a strange bird and my dad is blinded by his love for her. I think she has a spell on him."

"Well, let me get home before my mom gets off work. I'll text you later. You staying here tonight?"

Yes. I'm helping them in the community center tomorrow so I will see you there."

I closed the door gently behind Dylan. I changed my mind and decided to tell my Greats I was going home. I needed to talk to my mom. It sounded weird but being near her mural made me feel like she was still with me. I needed to be near her right now.

Chapter Twenty-five

I looked at the mail Maria placed on my bed. I was shaking. My hands trembled so bad; I had a hard time ripping open the envelope.

"AAAHHHHHHH!" I screamed to the top of my lungs. Maria ran into my room out of breath.

"What happened, Nina?"

"I got accepted to attend a STEM camp at Tuskegee University this summer and they offered me a scholarship to cover the two-week camp so I do not have to ask my dad or Nicole for the tuition cost!" I tumbled onto my bed, kicking my feet back and forth in the air.

"That's fantastic, Nina." Maria hugged me.

"Now, how many schools is that so far?" Maria asked me enthusiastically.

"This makes my first academic camp scholarship to a school. I got offers to three schools for volleyball camp, which is amazing but this one feels different because it's not for sports. This one reflects how hard I worked in school, and this is the one that would've made my mom proud." I held the letter close to my chest. Maria snuggled near me and hugged my shoulders when I sat on the bed.

"I think it's safe to say that your mother would be proud of you regardless. Nina, you came here and faced some tough challenges. I know I keep quiet because my job is to serve and not be heard, but you are one of the kindest kids I have ever experienced. You take the time out to treat me with respect and you never make me feel like the help. Nina, I didn't know your mother, but I can tell she was a great woman because she raised a great young woman. You're smart and you're tough and you have overcome so many obstacles without sacrificing your integrity."

"Well, Maria, I'm not perfect."

"None of us are." Maria kissed my forehead and then stood up to leave.

"Let me get going. I have a ton to do."

"Maria?"

"Yes, Nina?"

"Do you ever get tired?"

"Of what?"

"Being overworked and underappreciated?"

Maria didn't respond. She darted her eyes from me to her shoes. She smoothed out her uniform and walked out of my room, closing the door gently behind her.

"Mommy, look at this!" I ran to my closet to share the news.

"I got an academic STEM camp scholarship from Tuskegee, Mom! Isn't that awesome!"

"Nina, who are you talking to?" My back stiffened. I hurried to cover my mother's mural as Nicole was walking into my closet.

"I was talking to myself."

"Why do you have so much stuff bunched on that back wall when you have all this space in this closet."

"Oh, I have to organize it, but I know where everything is at."

"Whatever, you're a little sloppy for my taste, but any who, I was at the community center earlier today and your grandparents wanted me to remind you to make sure you remember the "read to me" event happening today. The event starts at three but there are parents already trickling into the center with their children."

"I'm getting ready to head down there now," she said. She flipped her wrist and left without another word. Typical Nicole, but what was not typical was her being in the community center instead of a shopping center on a beautiful Saturday afternoon.

I arrived at the community center a couple of hours later

but was still early. The place was already packed with parents. There were eight of us reading to the kids and two therapy dogs for the kids to read to them.

"Hey, Bryce, this is a great turn out." I was in a happy and cheerful mood.

"What are you bright eyed about? You came in here floating on your toes. What do you and Dylan have going on?"

"Me and Dylan?"

"Yeah, he spoke with your stepmom earlier and have been gloating from ear to ear ever since. You guys must be wrapping up prom details or something."

He spoke with my stepmom? What could she be speaking to him about?

"Believe it or not, he hasn't mentioned his senior prom yet. He's on the fence about going because of the cost. Right now, he's trying to figure out how to pay for his dream college since his SAT scores didn't land him the scholarship money he was banking on."

"Tell him to contact me if he needs help with trying to find money to help pay for school. There are tons of scholarships out there and he may have to work harder or write essays but there is still plenty of money on the table. Scores open doors which is why I stayed on you about studying and preparing for the SAT/ACT exams."

"Thank, Bryce," I said, giving her a hug. Her hugs always made me feel good. Dylan was standing across the room, so I made my way over toward him.

"Hey Babe, what's up?" Walking up to Dylan I spoke but didn't plan on mentioning what Bryce told me about him speaking to my stepmom. I wanted to see if he would tell me himself.

"Nothing, BK, just getting ready to read to the kiddos." Dylan's body language was stiff and rigid. He didn't have his usual swag.

"Everything good? You look stressed." I poked to see if he would reveal his conversation with my stepmother. I was curious what she said to him.

"Yeah, everything is all good. What about you? What's good?"

"Well, I got accepted to a two-week STEM camp at Tuskegee this summer on full scholarship!" I exclaimed.

"BK, that's awesome. How you get a scholarship though?"

"It was based on my grades," I responded, pissed that he asked about the scholarship versus the details of the program. Dylan knew I wanted to study veterinary medicine, and this was a huge deal for me since this was the only historically black university that offered this field of study.

"It seems like the people with money always get money thrown at them and the people in need never get anything."

"I'm not a person with money. My dad has money, but you already know that funnels through Nicole and does not flow freely to me. I busted my ass in school and my grades spoke to my academic commitment."

"True, but BK, you have to admit going to that fancy

private school is a plus."

"The Academy is a great school, but they do not give away grades, you have to earn them, and I busted my ass to earn mine."

"Calm down, Brooklyn, damn," Dylan chuckled, pulling me into his chest for a hug. I wasn't sure what he was implying but I was about to let him have it. The hug melted the tension and his cologne made me forget that he had just pissed me off. He kissed the top of my head and then the side of my face before releasing me.

"Let's go read to these bad ass kids. You at your Greats later? Can I roll through?" Dylan asked with a smile that gave me flutters.

"Of course, you can come through. Text me first so that I can make sure everything is all good."

Now that I had my own car, I was able to commute and stay with my Greats whenever I wanted to. Some weekdays, I commuted to school from their house. I loved the freedom of driving because this allowed me to spend more time with Dylan. Lately, he was beast mode with the dick, and I enjoyed every inch of him. I also got more involved with the community center and attached to a couple of the kids who attended regularly. I helped Bryce with creating different curriculums and events because she told me it looked great on my college resume.

Chapter Twenty-six

"Can you read me a book? I want to read this book right here," a little girl asked, tugging on my shirt.

"Absolutely. This is what the event is about. I would love to read you a book. Let's sit on the carpet crisscross applesauce."

The little girl was adorable. I decided to read the book in the most animated way possible.

"What is your name, pretty girl?"

"Kimberly," her tiny voice said.

"Kimberly, that is absolutely beautiful. May I call you Kim?"

"Sure, everybody calls me Kim."

"Ok, Kim. Once upon a time, there was a beautiful little

girl. Who lived in the castle?"

I felt sick to my stomach out of nowhere.

"Excuse me." I jumped up abruptly and ran to the bathroom. Everyone froze and looked up at me burst through the bathroom door where I started hurling over the trashcan.

"Nina, is everything okay?"

"Yes, Bryce, everything is fine. I don't know what happened. I feel so sick right now."

I leaned over and threw up again.

"Let me get you a napkin and put some cold water on it."

Bryce dabbed my face and looked at me with concern.

"You don't look too good. I think you should go home."

"Honestly, my head is spinning." I could barely stand up. I couldn't drive home like this.

"I don't think I'll be able to drive home. Let me just sit in the bathroom for a minute and gather myself. I feel awful right now."

I stumbled into the corner stall and sat on top of the toilet fully clothed. My head felt heavy, so I rested it in the palm of my hands. I wasn't sure what was happening, but I heard the bathroom stall door open.

"Nina?"

"Yeah."

"Come on, let me help you up. I'm going to take you to your grandparents. I'll stop at the store on the way there and buy you a ginger ale to help settle your stomach."

"Okay."

We stopped at CVS before Bryce took me to my grandparents' house. Once we arrived, Bryce helped me to my room.

"What do you think could be the problem? Was it something you ate?"

"Honestly, I'm not sure. I really haven't eaten anything today. However, the doctor said I'm anemic so that might have something to do with why I feel sick. I have to do better about eating and taking my iron pills." I rubbed my stomach in a circular motion and winched in pain.

"Well, to be on the safe side, I got you some stuff from the drugstore. Lay down and get some rest. When you feel better, there's items in this bag. Make sure you text me later. It's important that I know that you're good. Your grandparents will be here as soon as the event is over. They told me that they will call your dad and let him know that you will be hanging out with them for the night."

"Thanks, Bryce, I appreciate it." Bryce rubbed my arm then left.

I woke up to the smell of collard greens. I looked at the

clock and four hours had passed, and it was now early evening. I got up to go to the bathroom.

"Nina? Is that you? Are you up?" my Grandpa Mario yelled from downstairs.

"Yeah, I'm up."

"You want something to eat? Your grandma's been cooking. She can fix you something and I bring it up to you."

"That would be awesome, Grandpa. I'm in the bathroom now. Can you give me about ten minutes?"

"Sure, I'll be up in about ten to fifteen minutes."

I looked in the goodie bag Bryce left, hoping some sort of headache medicine was in the bag. My head was throbbing. I gasped when I saw the contents. Not only was there headache medicine but there was a pregnancy test, crackers, and a can of ginger ale. I grabbed my phone to text Bryce.

Thank you so much for bringing me to my greats' house. Thanks for my goodie bag. But a pregnancy test?

I looked at the bubbles. Bryce was responding quick. I was curious as to what she was going to say.

You're welcome. I was concerned, you didn't look well. The test is just a precaution. I slipped that in there because I want you to take it. I know you and Dylan are active and I know you are very cautious, but you just never know. Let me know. Ping me later.

My body went rigid.

I'm pretty sure that test... it will not be positive. I'm super safe and we always use condoms but thank you for thinking of me.

I'll touch base with you later. Goodnight

I sat on the edge of the bed. I threw the test in the bottom drawer of the nightstand. I opened my ginger ale, sipped on it, and heard my Greats talking as they were coming up the stairs.

"Hey Grandpa. Hey Grandma."

"Hey, baby, how are you feeling?" my grandma asked with concerned eyes.

"A little bit better. Bryce bought me a ginger ale that I'm sipping on here."

"I made sure I cooked some really good food for you. You probably are exhausted cause you haven't been eating and you've been running all over, practicing and playing volleyball nonstop."

"You're probably right, Grandma, thank you much."

She placed a dinner tray over my lap. I backed up and scooted to the headboard.

"Let me feel your head for a fever," my grandma said.

"You feel a little warm," she said. "Maybe you're coming down with a cold. You slept a long time."

"I'm not sure about a cold but I feel a little bit better and I'm sure I'll be fine once I eat your dinner."

"Okay, go slow. We're gonna go clean up the kitchen and you just holler at us when you need us."

"Thank you, I love you guys."

I smiled when I looked at my food. The plate was sectioned so that my food wouldn't touch. The smell of the food made me nauseous. I got up, ran to the bathroom, and threw up again.

What the hell is wrong with me? I'm starving. My grandparents' food never makes me sick. After I threw up, I wiped off the toilet seat to use the bathroom. I looked down and saw a streak of blood in my panties. I was shocked and decided to take the pregnancy test. After waiting a few minutes, I looked at the results. I dropped the stick on the floor.

I was pregnant.

Chapter Twenty-seven

The grey skies illuminated through the basement windows of my great grandparents' house. My mind was a million miles away, while Dylan stood in front of me talking. It was just words; I wasn't retaining any of it.

Pregnant. God why is this happening to me? I did the very thing that I promised myself and my mother's spirit that I would never do. I allowed myself to become a underaged, uneducated mother.

My heart was breaking because I was at a crossroad. As much as I wanted to be a mother one day, I always thought it would be far in the future. I wanted motherhood to come with a great husband, who proved that he loved me so much, that I would bestow the highest honor by giving him a baby. The pain of not having my father in my life, I wanted to make sure that history didn't repeat itself. It wouldn't be so bad if I was unmarried and, in a position, to take care of myself and a baby but that wasn't the case. I wasn't old enough to rent a car, register to vote, or rent an apartment. I didn't have any credit, except one credit card with a five-hundred-dollar limit that was tied to my dad's account.

All I had at this point was my opportunity to get an education. That was my out. That was the only exit strategy that I had planned. Things may have been different if this was happening under my mother's roof. Although she would've been disappointed, she would've supported me. Between her, Ms. Alba, and myself this baby would've had more than enough love, but that was never going to happen. My mother was dead and as painful as it has been for me to accept it, that fact was anchored in my family's history.

"You can't do that! What are you talking about, BK? You can't get rid of our baby."

"What am I talking about? What the hell are you talking about, Dylan? We're both trying to go to college. You're graduating in a few months. I'm graduating next year. I play volleyball and looking at a scholarship offers. There are several schools interested in me! My father will kill me. My mother will rise from her grave to fuck me up and then re-bury herself! My great grandparents will be extremely disappointed. How am I going to have a baby, Dylan? We have to get up some money and discreetly abort this baby. That's our only option."

"Nina, that's not fair. I want the baby. I really need you to have this baby. It's a part of me. It probably will be good for both of us." I wrinkled my nose and my mouth fell open. Dylan complained so much about how much his mother worked. How she never spent time with him and how he felt like he was at a disadvantage from not having his father in his life. Dylan sat right here in the basement of my Greats' house on several occasions teary eyed expressing how hard it was to watch his mom struggle and worked around the clock. It made me dizzy to think that he was going to put me and this baby in that same situation.

Yes, Dylan and I loved each other but I was no fool. I knew that it was puppy love. It felt good and it felt real but was it everlasting? I wasn't that naïve. Dylan would go to college and his world would explode with tons of female opportunities. What freshman male wanted to be locked down with a high school girlfriend on a HBCU campus filled with beautiful women. I even wondered if it would be best that we broke up to enjoy college then wait to see what life had in store for us after college. I hadn't had the chance to have that conversation with Dylan, but I was going to offer him an out or a break during college. I looked at Dylan because I thought his reaction was based off his emotions and he wasn't thinking clearly.

"Dylan, do you hear what you are saying? You're talking crazy. How in the hell will a baby be good for a seventeen and an eighteen-year-old, unmarried, unstable, no job having couple?" I wondered if Dylan was on drugs at this point.

"Nina, I know it will be tough, but you have your parents."

"Are you fucking kidding me? My parents? Have you lost your mind, Dylan? My mother is dead. My father is so out of touch; he's barely a part of his own family, let alone a father to me. And my stepmother a.k.a step-monster is completely fucking crazy!"

"Nina. I don't think your stepmother is that bad."

"Huh? What the fuck did you just say to me? After all the shit I told you she has put me through. Are you on drugs right now?" This time I flat out asked him because this was unbelievable. This was not the Dylan that swept me off my feet and dreamed out loud with me on the floor of my Greats' basement for the past couple of years. This was not the Dylan who I gave my heart to and in return he gave me comfort and love and made me feel valued when I felt no value in my home. I wasn't sure who this was in front of me, but he was a stranger.

"Nina. Let's just take a moment and think about this. I think we should take a few days to think about what we're saying here. This is a huge decision. Look, I gotta run. Take care of yourself. I'll see you tomorrow, okay? I have to make sure I get home before my mom gets in from work." He kissed me on the lips, but I didn't return the sentiment.

"You see, this is what I mean right here. You have to run home before your mom comes home. What if this baby was sick during the middle of the night? What if I had to run him or her to the emergency room? What would happen then? Would it just be on me to figure it all out? Are you prepared to stay home and go to community college so that you can be a dad? At the end of the day, BOTH of our lives will change drastically not just mine." Dylan froze but was unable to give me eye contact.

"Dylan, do you understand the magnitude of what you're saying." I grabbed Dylan's face gently to force eye contact.

"I gotta go, BK," he said before he released my hands and walked out the door.

I stood against the door after I locked it. Dylan's behavior baffled me. What was he talking about? He was delusional if he thought I was going to have this baby. I needed to figure out a way to get rid of this baby before anyone even knew that I was pregnant. The only person I could call on was Bryce. I had my fingers crossed she would help me deal with this situation. Once I got home and calmed my nerves, I was going to reach out to her. It would be a huge ask but since Dylan wasn't on board, she was all I had.

Chapter Twenty-eight

"Nina, wake up, honey. We need to talk." I was extremely tired. When I looked up, my dad and Nicole were looking down at me. My dad's eyes were sad. Nicole was standing with her arms crossed.

"What's going on?" I asked.

"Nina, we spoke to Dylan, and he told us you're pregnant." My dad eyes were pleading like he wanted this truth to be a lie. I gasped for air; I felt like someone gut punched me.

"What?"

"He told us you're pregnant which is why you have been sluggish and lazy and sleeping more than usual." My eyes darted toward Nicole; she was pointing her finger at me and smirking while she spoke.

Stunned. I couldn't speak. I saw Nicole's mouth moving, but her words were muffled like she was underwater. My dad sat quietly.

"I have already talked to your coach because it is no longer safe for you to play. Ryan and Riley agreed to let you take turns carpooling with them to school because we believe it is no longer safe for you to drive. You can barely stay awoke here lately."

"What?" This situation went from zero to one hundred faster than I could comprehend.

"During our family meeting, Maria discussed with us all the schools that offered you scholarships which you will have to decline. You will have to sit out a few years or try to go to a local community college so that you can take care of the baby." Nicole was speaking like she was in a business meeting. She talked about my future plans like I cared about her input or what she thought.

"Family meeting? Dad what is she talking about?" I ignored her and wanted to talk to the only person I shared blood with. Speaking over him, Nicole kept talking like he wasn't there. My dad sat still like a fucking rock. Nicole would love nothing more than to gloat about my misstep, she had the audacity to assume I wanted to keep this baby.

"Nina, once I found out the news, I gathered everyone in the family so we can sort out how to move forward. This is a major situation, and your actions will affect the whole family. We have never had to deal with an out of wedlock, underage pregnancy before, but we will get through it." Nicole never looked up from her phone.

"I'm not pregnant!" The lie rolled off my tongue.

"What? Are you sure? Nicole told me that Dylan told her you were," my dad said, straightening his back.

"Since when are you and Dylan friends? Why would he tell you that?" I asked Nicole.

"I make sure to be friends with anyone who dates one of my daughters," Nicole said with fake concern

"Since when? Since when have you cared about who I date? Since when have you cared about anything that happens to me?" I was at the end of my rope.

"Nina, let's all come down," my dad said. He hated for anyone to get in his wife's ass. He made me sick.

"Nina, that's fatigue talking. I experienced the same things during all three of my pregnancies." Nicole fanned her hand over her face, dismissing my questions.

"I am not pregnant!" I yelled.

"Okay, just to be sure we got a pregnancy test here. Why don't you go in the bathroom and pee on the stick?" Nicole challenged me.

"I ain't peeing on shit for you," I challenged back, looking her square in the eye.

"Okay, well, I pulled some strings and got you an OB/GYN appointment. Nina, I don't see why Dylan would lie. If he is, then shame on him." Nicole hunched her shoulders and leaned against the wall.

"We will find out at your appointment. If you're pregnant, we need to take proper measures to assure a safe and healthy baby is welcomed into this family. We want you to know that although we are extremely disappointed, we will support you. The school will support you as well and you can continue to study at the Academy, or we can transfer you into a school for pregnant girls."

"You contacted my school? Why would you have a family meeting? What would make you do any of those things without talking to me first?"

"Honey, I know that Nicole may have jumped the gun, but she is looking at what's best for you."

"No, she's not. Why does she have sole control over everything in your damn house! I am not pregnant!"

"Nina, this is her house too and you better start respecting your mom a little better than you have here lately! We are only trying to help. We both love you."

"Can you guys leave my room please?" My insides were an inferno. If my dad referred to her as my mom one more time, I was going bash his skull with the lamp on my nightstand.

"Honey, don't be upset with us. Having sex comes with consequences. Dylan said he would step up and do what he can to support the baby. Although he will be away at Morehouse, he promises to come home as much as possible to visit and spend time with the baby." Nicole sounded insincere and rehearsed.

"Morehouse? How do you know he's going to Morehouse?"

"He told me," Nicole said blankly, raising her palms in the air and hunching her shoulders.

How in the world is he going to Morehouse?

"Nina, I know it's a tough pill to swallow. He gets to enjoy his college life on campus and your college experience will look different, but this is the sacrifice us mothers have to make sometimes." The look on Nicole's face made me want to slap her. Maria was raising her kids.

"Can you guys leave please!" I rubbed my temples. I was seeing red. I wanted to strangle the life out of Dylan with my bare hands.

"Nina—" my dad started.

"LEAVE!"

My dad patted my shoulder and walked away. Nicole looked down at me expressionless, rolled her eyes, and walked away.

I rushed to get my phone off the charger. I needed to call Dylan because he lost his motherfucking mind. Everything started to swirl, and my emotions were all over the place. I felt weak before I blacked out.

Chapter Twenty-nine

The smell of disinfectant swarmed my nose. The beeps, constant voices, and bright lights made me look around and squint my eyes. Everything was foggy and my arm was throbbing.

I was in a hospital room.

"Everything will be fine. Santina is severely dehydrated, and her iron is low. She needs rest. We will start her on prenatal pills and give her an iron supplement. She's about four weeks pregnant and this is a very sensitive stage in her journey. We want her to take precautions to assure a healthy pregnancy," the doctor said to my dad.

"Thank you, doctor," my dad spoke low.

The bright lights hurt my eyes. I saw a big window overlooking the hospital parking lot that backed against a major street. I counted the cars as they drove by on the highway below while I felt a soft hand rubbing my hairline. My mouth felt like cotton and my throat felt raw. Staring up, I saw my dad. The soft hand was Nicole's. I jerked my head and removed her hand. I tried sitting up.

"Lay down and try to relax. Don't get up. We don't want you getting dizzy again," my dad said, pressing gently on my shoulders.

"You fainted and took a hard fall, but the baby is fine. We made sure the doctors ran test and confirmed," Nicole spoke low with her hands clasped. A lone tear ran down my face.

"Confirmed?" I asked.

"Yes. He confirmed that you are indeed pregnant, and we are going to do whatever we can to support you," Nicole gloated.

Damn. This is not how I wanted this to play out. Now my dad and Nicole knew my secret. The door opened. Ryan, Riley, and Addison of all fucking people entered my room.

"Hey, Nina, how are you feeling?" Riley smiled, walking toward me.

"Hey, Nina," Ryan came next.

"Hey, Nina, we heard you weren't well and wanted to come check on you. The team was concerned," Addison screeched. That bitch.

"The team? How does the team even know I'm in the

hospital? I just got here two damn seconds ago."

"Oh, we were told in the team group chat by your sisters. Everyone signed a card for you, Nina. We are going to be sad that you can't play on the team." Addison handed me a card, but I didn't reach for it. Nicole took it and placed it on my stomach.

"Thank you so much, Addison. Nina will need the love and support of all of you. This is a very kind gesture."

I snatched the card off my stomach, ripped it up, and threw it at Addison's feet. She had her phone and out like she was about to snap a photo or record.

"I wish your ass would." I stared at her with cold eyes. She put the phone up.
The door swung open again. It was Dylan.

"Hey everybody," he said shyly.

Seeing his face gave me mixed emotions. I watched and studied him carefully. He smiled from ear to ear like he hit the fucking lotto and hugged Nicole. He went to shake my dad's hand and my dad crossed his arms around his midsection and stared him down without saying a word.

"Uh, Nina, look who's here to see you?" Nicole was trying to break up the tension. The room felt heavy. The air was stale and felt smoggy like a humid summer day.

"I see him!" I snapped.

"How you feel, Nina?" My dad walked to my bed and shifted his weight from one leg to another.

"Um, let's clear the room so Nina and Dylan can talk. I'm

sure they want some privacy," Nicole stated. Everyone got up to leave except my dad.

"Come on, honey. Let the kids have privacy. I'm sure they have a lot to talk about," Nicole pleaded with my dad. He ignored her and kept his eyes fixated on Dylan.

"Dad," I called, watching him stare Dylan down.

"Yes, dear," he responded without moving or giving me eye contact. He was piercing through Dylan's soul.

"Both you and Dylan can leave now. I just want to be by myself." Dylan looked up from his sneakers.

"Wait, before you both leave, I have a question."

"Sure, honey, what's up?" my dad responded with a tone that made Dylan take two steps back.

"Dylan, is it true that you're going to Morehouse?"

"Uh yeah." He couldn't look at me.

"How are you able to afford Morehouse? That private school is expensive, and you told me that the FASFA didn't offer you enough money to be able to attend?"

"I got a sponsor, with everything that has been going on and things moving so fast I didn't get a chance to tell you about this program that I am in that helps low-income youth pay for college. I got sponsored and they will pay my tuition." Dylan beamed with pride. I looked at him expressionless.

"It's funny you never mentioned this program to me."

"I know, I mean things have been moving so fast and with the sudden pregna—" I saw my dad cringe when Dylan spoke those words. I cut him off.

"I see or talk to you every single day, Dylan."

"I know but it happened so fast, I was going to tell you last week."

"You had to be in this program longer than a week?"

"Um, em, I got involved around..." Dylan looked at his feet dumbfounded. He stuttered then paused like he was stuck on stupid. He was lying to me, and I wasn't in the mood. I wasn't interested in whatever lie he was trying to sell me. I cut his words off again.

"Goodbye, Dylan. Daddy, you both can go now. I would like to get some rest," I said, touching his arm gently to break his trance.

"Alright, Nina, I'll give you a couple of hours to yourself to get some rest. I'll be back. You should be released in the morning. They just want to keep you for observation overnight." My dad leaned in and kissed my forehead.

They made their way to the door. Dylan was in front and swung it open. I looked toward the door and saw Nicole standing right in front of it looking in.

Nosey ass

I shook my head and turned over to lay down. I knew her ass hadn't gone too far. It didn't surprise me that she was glued to the door the whole time.

Delia Rouse

Chapter Thirty

I felt like my world was crashing down around me. The things I endured was so unfair to me and I hated it here in this thing called life. Everything was dark and I couldn't find comfort to sooth my soul. My Greats were a source of light but even their love couldn't erase the pain and betrayal I experienced. I felt lifeless. The humiliation and embarrassment were at an all-time high and I wanted to vanish into thin air, shoot like a cannonball above the clouds, land in heaven to meet my mother at the altar so that I could apologize for letting her down as a daughter.

There was a knock at the door. *Dammit! I can't have a private moment in the hospital...what part of I need some alone time don't these people understand?*

My Greats and Bryce walked into my room. My Greats looked exhausted. I never considered how my behavior would take a toll on them. My grandma rushed to my bedside and didn't speak a word. She placed her soft cheek against mine and droplets left her eyes and landed on my face. I relaxed once I felt her rub my arm up and down.

My grandpa strolled to the other side of the bed and grabbed my hand. His calloused hand squeezed mine. My eyes tightened and I tried to stop my tears from falling but failed. This was what I needed, their light and love.

"Look a here, sweetheart," my great-grandfather's booming voice was as soft as he could make it.

"We love you no matter what you got going on."

"We sure do," Bryce stated.

When I was brave enough to give eye contact, I followed the echo of that last statement, which led me to Bryce standing at the foot of my hospital bed. She rubbed my foot through the thin sheet.

"I'm sorry, guys," I whispered.

"You have nothing to be sorry for. We were all young once and we have all made choices that we sometimes regret." My great-grandmother was sitting beside me on the edge of the bed, holding my hand for dear life. It was nice to remember what love felt like.

"I'm not sure about having a baby." My voice was a little shaky.

"Look here now…. I know me and your great grandma is old, but we will help you as best we can with the little one. Don't let anyone make you feel bad for being a young mother. Your grandma and I were young parents too and we had no idea what we were doing with your grandfather, but he turned out alright."

"Grandpa Mario, eighties is the new sixty. You guys are not that old."

"That's not what my body says when it's about to rain, or when it's cold and good ole Mr. Arthur Rithis visits me." My grandpa was the only person I knew that referred to his arthritis like it was a person with a first and last name.

"Honey, I'm going to tell you something. Your grandpa and I have made our own lives without the direction of what others thought. We have seen it all and we have done it all. There is nothing that you should be ashamed of."

"Grandma, you guys have been married sixty-four years; you started a family young, but you were still married. I am not even out of high school. I was really enjoying my team and looking forward to prom. I wanted to play volleyball in college and live on campus, I wanted to pledge a sorority and be a regular student"

"Nina, you can still do all of those things. It may look different and be a little tougher, but it can still be accomplished." Bryce walked to the front of my bed and stood closer to my grandmother.

"I just can't see going back to school now. Everyone knows

I'm pregnant thanks to my sisters and their big mouths."

"Nicole was looking into a high school for mothers. Maybe that will be a better environment for you since everyone will be in the same situation," my grandpa stated.

"You know something, Grandpa. Nicole talks too much! She took this news and ran with it. Why would she do that knowing how extremely private this is?" I was leaning up on my forearms. The sound of her name made steam come out of my nostrils.

"I think she's excited," my grandma exclaimed.

"I don't think so," I stated. Bryce gave me a knowing look.

My Greats leaned in to snuggle me before leaving.

"Baby, we are going to head out. We'll be checking in on you. we love you," my Grandma Diane said.

"I know you do, and I love you guys too."
Bryce hugged them but stayed planted in her spot. Once the door closed, she turned to me and smiled.

"Okay, doll. Talk to me. What's up? How you really feeling?"

Sighing deeply, I was glad she asked. I wanted to unload my mental burdens on her because I trusted her with my thoughts.

"I feel so alone and confused."

"Why alone? I am here your grandparents are here your dad, siblings. What's causing these feelings?"

"Something is off, and I don't know what it is. You know my stepmother is all about her family image and now she acts like she's ecstatic that I'm pregnant. Where's the chastising? Where's the punishment for having underage sex? My dad isn't saying it, but I can tell he's disappointed. This will sound weird, but I think Nicole is happy that I got caught out there. She even had a family meeting! She has already spoke to my school administrators. She didn't even give me the chance to sit in my situation and have a private moment."

"You think she is trying to humiliate you?"

"I am not sure. My biggest shock is Dylan. I thought he was different. I thought we were so close, and I feel betrayed. Why would he tell Nicole after I told him I didn't want to have this baby? I can't understand it knowing that she has been the source of my pain since I moved here. I have cried on his shoulders on several occasions, and he knows how I feel about her. Why would he betray me by telling her? I feel like a fool."

"Well, honey, I know this is going to be hard to hear but take it from me a woman who has been around the block once or twice. Men sometimes just ain't shit. They create a shit storm and then they walk away, leaving us to pick up the pieces."

"Dylan was so awesome to me. He really acted like he cared. He was the first boy that connected with me and made me feel loved. We even planned events for the kids at the community center together and talked about tutoring strategies and how we would mentor kids who needed a big brother or sister to talk to. I honestly thought he was different."

"Boys sometimes will be whatever you need them to be

when they want sex from you, honey. That's just how they are wired."

"I do not understand why Dylan didn't tell me he was in this sponsorship program. How long has he been in it? We both planned on what schools we were going to, and Morehouse was way out of his reach. Now, magically, he's going?"

"Did he say what the name of the program was? I can call around and find out more about it. You know my fraternity brothers are in some of everything when it comes to sponsoring youth. Do you know the name of the program?"

"Yes, he said it was called Upward Bound."

Bryce pulled her phone from her purse and texted ferociously.

"What do you want to do, Nina?"

"What do you mean?"

"I mean exactly what I said. Nina is in control of Nina's destiny. Tell me what you want to do with the cards you have been dealt?"

I had to think for a moment. I looked down at my fingers and before I could speak the nurse walked into my room.

"Hey there. It's time for me to check your vitals." Her whimsical voice irritated me because nurses always came at the worst times.

Bryce stood up.

"Don't leave," I said abruptly.

"I'm not going anywhere. I'm going to step outside and let

her handle her business. I'll come back once she is done."

"Is that your big sister?" the nurse asked, smiling wide.

"I wish," I said, meaning it.

Delia Rouse

Chapter Thirty-one

After two days of monitoring me, I was discharged from the hospital. I was dehydrated and my iron was low. I was prescribed prenatal pills, iron pills, and a referred to an OB/GYN to start prenatal care. Bryce spent a tremendous amount of time with me during my hospital stay. We talked a lot and she made me realize that I was a minor and would need parental consent to get an abortion and adoption may have been an alternative for me. I wasn't sure how I felt about carrying a baby just to give it away. It was a lose-lose situation. I just wanted to get home, shower, and relax so that I could think.

My dad picked me up from the hospital alone which shocked me. I thought of all the times I wished I had him to myself and now that we were in the car together, I couldn't find my voice.

"You ready to go home, baby?"

"Yes, Dad."

"We're happy to have you back home. How do you feel? We all missed you."

"Daddy, I was only in the hospital a few days. I feel fine."

"Well, a few days felt like a lifetime. We're excited that you are healthy and coming home. Nicole has something special for you at the house." My dad beamed, looking from the road to me and then back on the road. I looked at him, tilting my head sideways. I couldn't begin to imagine what his wife had planned for me.

"The doctors said everything looked good. They said if you wanted someone to talk to about your situation, they could give us a referral."

"Someone to talk to like a shrink?"

"Yeah, I mean you are going through a lot and if you need someone to talk to then I don't mind paying for you to see someone. Nicole mentioned that she was concerned for you and didn't want you hurting yourself or the baby. Nina, this is not the ideal way I wanted to become a grandpa, but I do understand that things happen, and I don't want anything to happen to you. I have already lost your mother." I scoffed under my breath.

"Daddy, I'm fine. I do not need to see anyone."

"Okay, but in case you ever do just let me know." My dad patted me on my leg as we drove the rest of the way, humming to the radio. I sat in silence. I wondered why my dad would rather pay for me to talk to someone than to talk to me himself.

I dreaded walking into the house when we pulled into the driveway. I didn't want to deal with my father's wife or her damn kids. The landscaping was immaculate. The curb appeal was warm and inviting. I felt the complete opposite inside of the dwelling.

"Welcome home!"

My family greeted me when I entered. I was underwhelmed. There were balloons everywhere and a sign with my name. Nicole ran up and hugged me but I hugged her back like she was contagious. She grabbed my hand and walked me in front of the family like I was on display.

"Everybody, let's love on Nina. She has been through a lot, and we want to show her how much we love her and support her through her motherhood journey."

I felt sick to my stomach. Nicole turned to look me in the eyes, while holding my shoulders.

"I want you to know that we all care about you and we all will stand by you and support you one hundred percent. We have a huge surprise for you." My brows furrowed. I couldn't imagine what kind of surprise she had for me. My dad smiled behind her proudly.

"Come everyone, let's go upstairs!" she yelled. Everyone migrated to the steps. Looking around at all the giddy smiling faces, I felt like I was in the twilight zone. This was getting stranger by the moment.

Everyone hustled upstairs and they stopped in front of my closed room door.

"What's going on, guys?" my voice cracked.

"Let's go inside," Nicole said, opening my room door.

I walked in slowly and looked around. Everything seemed normal except for Maria straightening my room. It was spotless. I wasn't sure what Nicole was up to.

"Come in everyone." Everyone smiled and gathered inside of my room, making me extremely uncomfortable.

"Nina, we wanted to all chip in and do something nice for you," my dad interrupted her.

"Baby girl, it was all Nicole's idea. We hope you like it. But before we present it, put this on." My dad walked over and placed a blindfold over my face.

"Dad, is this necessary?" I asked, knowing I hated surprises.

"Yes, baby, we want you to be surprised." My dad grabbed my hand and walked me toward what seemed like my bathroom, I shuffled my feet so I wouldn't fall.

"I got you. Come on, honey."

I heard squeals and whispers. I then heard Nicole saying sshh. "Okay, honey. On the count of three take off her eye mask. One ...two...three."

"Surprise!" everyone yelled.

I blinked fast and looked around. I was not in my

bathroom; I was in my walk-in closet. My heart dropped. I gazed around the area in a panic from side to side and saw a crib and matching changing table was in my small alcove while my clothes were moved into the larger space in the closet. There was a small glider and matching foot stool.

My head felt heavy. It smelled of strong acrylic paint. I gripped my dad's arm because my legs felt like they were rubber. My cheeks were on fire and my heart rate accelerated.

"Do you like it, dear?" Nicole asked in a fabricated motherly tone while she had her hands clasped in front of her chest.

I glared at her and then at the smooth pink and pale grey painted accent wall. The chevron pattern made me dizzy. I snapped.

I lunged for Nicole and slapped her across the face, swiping the smirk off. I scratched and punched her, while she shielded herself.

My father and grandfather grabbed me, but my feet and arms were in full swing. I kicked my grandpa, knocking him into the small nightstand, which caused the porcelain elephant lamp to shatter against the wall and flood the carpet with shards of glass.

My dad grabbed me in a bear hug, but I extended my legs, propelling them like a motorized fan. I kicked Nicole in the chin. When she leaned over to cover her face, blood spewed from her mouth. Riley and Ryan ran to her, throwing daggers my way.

"Nina! Nina! Stop what the hell is wrong with you?" my

dad yelled at me with wild eyes, tossing me against the wall violently.

"This is the fucking thanks my wife gets for going out of her way to create a nursery for your underage pregnant ass!"

"Your wife is a bitch! I hate her! I hate her!" I screamed.

My grandmas ran over to me and tried and to get me up from the wall. I was slumped over crying the hardest tears I've ever cried.

"Nina, baby. What's wrong? We thought you would love the baby nursery. We scrambled to get it together in such a short amount of time," my grandma asked in the gentlest tone she could muster. Looking into her eyes, I saw her wrinkles creased around her pupils.

"Two years! Two years I worked on my mother's mural that was on that wall and in two days Nicole took her away from me all over again."

Nicole was crying and holding her face, while Ryan and Riley dabbed her ripped flesh with cotton balls. She assessed her face in the wall mirror. The bloody beet faced monster turned to me and swore.

"I had no idea that it was a painting of your mother. I thought it was some form of ghetto street art you painted on the walls. Forgive me for trying to do something nice and create a welcoming space for your baby. I really thought I was doing something that would make you happy."

I threw a small, ceramic elephant bank from the nightstand.

Nicole ducked and the bank shattered against the wall.

"Get out!" Nicole screamed.

"I want this ungrateful bitch daughter of yours out! I'm scared for my life and she's unstable." She fell into her husband's arms and wailed like a dying animal.

"Grandma, Pops," my dad whispered to his grandparents.

"Is it okay if Nina stays with you while I find a way to get her help?"

And just like that my dad chose sides.

Chapter Thirty-two

It had been a week since I was back at my Greats. I wanted to ask them if I could stay with them permanently but thought better of it because that would've been selfish of me. My Greats were too old to be catering to me and a newborn baby and my Grands were too young to be catering to me and a newborn. Plus, I hadn't grown as close to them and would feel weird invading their space. My Grandpa Richard was a pastor and my Grandma Sabrina treated being a first lady like a full-time job. They traveled, entertained, and were socialites so asking to stay with them was uncomfortable for me.

"Nina, you have to get out of bed, honey. Don't you want to eat something?"

"Grandma, I'm not hungry."

"Honey, you have to feed the baby. You have to try, please eat something."

"Okay, Grandma. I'll try." My grandma placed a tray of food down. I knew I wasn't going to eat it because I didn't have an appetite. I didn't want to eat. I didn't want to get out of my bed. I didn't want to bathe. All I wanted was to lay in bed and be alone.

When I looked up at the ceiling, tears fell down the sides of my face. That bitch, Nicole, found my mother's mural and painted over it on purpose. I knew she did. If Nicole didn't know anything else, she knew exactly what my mother looked like. She knew that was a picture of her. I felt in my heart she did that with malice. The action alone was confirmation. I hated her and I hated my dad for marrying her. I hated my siblings for being created inside of her. They could all rot in hell.

There was a knock at my bedroom door.

"Hey, sweetheart. It's your Grandpa Mario. Can I come in?"

I forced myself to push down a forkful of grits. I bit a piece of bacon and then yelled for him to come in.

"Hey Grandpa Mario." He looked concerned, and I felt horrible because I knew it was because of me.

"How you doing?" My grandfather raised his glasses to his forehead when he asked that.

"I am okay."

"We are headed down to the community center in a little while and wanted you to come along. We think the fresh air would do you good and it's beautiful outside today."

"No, you and Grandma go ahead. I don't want to go."

"Nina, it's been one week since you have been here, and you have not left this room."

"I know, Grandma. I just don't feel like dealing with the outside world yet. I enjoy being by myself right now."

The doorbell chimed, interrupting our conversation.

"You expecting company, Diane? No, not that I am aware of." My grandpa walked out of my room and went to get the door.

"Grandma, I hope I am not putting you out by staying here with you and Grandpa. You do not have to cook for me every day."

"Chile, I cook every day for me and Mario anyway, so it's not a big deal. It's just a matter of making one extra plate. You know me and your grandpa don't like eating out too much. My food is much healthier, and I don't know if people wash their hands or their vegetables good now a days. You're not a bother at all, get that out of your head. I adore every moment with you."

"Hey, Nina. How are you feeling today?" my grandmother stopped, and my dad entered the room. "Let's open up some blinds and get some sun in here." My dad waltzed around, opening blinds, and letting the sunrays beam into my space. The windows sparkled from the sunrays, and it looked like he had a halo around him as he stood in front of the window facing me.

"Nina, I found a great therapist for you to talk to. Your sessions start this week. Nicole made arrangements for your new high school and all your transcripts are transferred so you will start there next week. Once you get a grip on your anger then we can talk about getting you back in the family home."

Quiet… I stared at him blankly… I was trying to find out what did my mom ever see in him. He was weak, whipped, and pathetic. Nicole's personal worshipper.

"Nina, did you hear what I said?"

"Yep."

"How do you feel about what I proposed?"

"I don't." I snapped my head in his direction and his eyes widened.

"Come here for a moment, Grandson. Let me speak with you," my grandma commanded.

I watched her pull my dad outside of the room. I had no idea what they whispered about, but I was happy she got him out of my face. He made me want to puke. A few moments later, my dad walked back into the room.

"Baby girl, I will come back and check on you in a few days. We can talk about this then. Right now, just rest and get well. I love you." He kissed my forehead. I didn't say a word back. I looked at him like he was a clown. He turned around and walked back out my room door.

My grandma came back into the room and sat on my bed.

"I could tell he was getting on your nerves, baby. He was getting on my nerves, so I asked him to go. Plus, I could tell Nicole was getting antsy sitting in the car."

"Does he do anything without her?"

"Nah, chile, you know that's his shadow," my grandpa said, chuckling from the doorway.

"What's so funny, Mario?" my grandma snapped.

"I can't get over the way Nina beat her ass in the baby's nursery. Whew, that was funny to me.... Nicole never saw that beat down coming." My grandma and I chuckled. I shook my head as sadness came over me. Someone rang the door and Grandpa Mario went to answer it.

"Hey, Chica," Bryce greeted.

"Hey, Bryce."

"How we doing today?"

"I'm doing."

"Well, I have an idea that I think would boost your spirits and make you smile."

"Really? What could that be?"

"Well, keep an open mind when I tell you. I spoke with your Greats and got permission from your dad."

"Huh? You spoke to my dad? When?"

"Just now, I ran into him walking out of the house. Hear me out a second."

"Okay.... but I can already tell I won't like it"

"Have you ever scrapbooked?"

"Yes, a long time ago. I used to scrapbook with my live-in nanny, Alba, to preserve my mother's memories after she passed and before I moved here."

"Well, let's do it again. What do you think about making a scrapbook or a shadow box of some of your favorite things of your mom or some of your favorite pictures? Maybe we can find a scarf or one of her sweaters and incorporate that somehow. I know it will not replace the mural that was painted over but at least you will have something of hers to look at daily."

"How are we going to do that?"

"Your dad gave me the key to the storage unit where your childhood house items are being stored. He didn't want it to be a trigger for you, but I told him I believe it would be therapeutic to go through your mom things and pick out some favorites for us to work with. You're creative and we can make something beautiful."

"Now, be honest if you don't think this is a good idea. I was trying to think of ways to get you out of this rut you're feeling."

"No! I think it's a great idea. I completely forgot that my dad had that storage unit. It's been so long."

"It's been a couple of years do you think you can handle seeing some of your mom's things? The last thing I want to do is get you deeper into a funk." Bryce touched my hand.

"I think it's a great idea. When can we go?" I jumped out of bed, looking for my socks and sneakers.

"Whoa...that's the most energy I've seen you exert since you played volleyball, young lady." My grandpa chuckled, holding his stomach. He was right. I was excited to explore this storage unit.

"Well, honey, your grandpa and I have something to do at the center. Is it okay if Bryce goes with you?"

"Yeah, Grandma that is fine."

"Yay!" Bryce threw her hands in the air and yelled.

"We can stop at the craft store once you pick out some things.

This will be awesome."

Delia Rouse

Chapter Thirty-three

My dad's storage unit was a massive enclosed four car garage bay. When I unlocked the side door to the unit, it gave me mixed emotions. I dropped the key twice.

"I got it." Bryce took the keys from me and let us inside.

I flipped on the lights, noticing my sectional from my bonus room and my mother's king-sized bed.

"I completely forgot that my stuff was this close to me. I never thought about what happen to the things from my home. I remember a truck coming with my clothes and some small items, but I assumed all the major stuff was destroyed in the truck accident during the move. "

"Some of it may have been lost but it looks like they savaged a lot of it. How big was your mother's home?" Bryce looked like she was exploring a consignment shop as she walked around, running her fingers along the sofa.

"It was a four-bedroom home. A nice size for us. Not as big as my dad's home. Maybe the size of my Greats."

"Nina, this is a decent amount of stuff. It looks like you will have a fully furnished home once you get your first place."

I ran my fingers across the back of my mother's dining room chair. They were stacked on top of each other. The metal studs made me think of her. She loved different metals. Harsh metals and delicate fabrics were her style.

"I spoke with your dad briefly, Nina," Bryce said out of the blue.

"Oh yeah, and what about?"

"I'm scared to say this, but I think he is genuinely concerned for you."

"Well, I think he is a genuine fool." Bryce chuckled and put her hand across her chest.

"Tell me why you honestly would think that?"

"Because he believes everything his wife says and does. You cannot tell me for one minute that she didn't paint that wall on purpose. I'm also not convinced that she didn't purposely leave me out of our family vacation when I first got here. Nicole is sinister and no one sees what I see."

"I'm not sure about all of those things, but I do think she can be petty. There is something about her that I don't like. She does walk around like she's the Queen of England or something.

But do you think she would really do those horrible things? Especially to a child who just lost her mother?"

"Honestly, I do. I think she hates me because I remind her of my mother. I think she is insecure and jealous of my mother because she was my dad's first love, and she gave him his first child."

"You may be right. I mean, she does like to pretend she has the perfect family. Maybe in her mind you disrupted that image." Bryce did air quotes.

"I just don't believe or trust anything about that lady. I'm so happy I will be out of their house in less than a year."

"Really. Realistically, where do you plan to go?" Bryce scrunched her eyebrows.

"I am glad you asked. I want an abortion."

"Huh? Aren't you like three months, Nina?"

"Yes. I'm almost three months and I want an abortion. I was trying to catch you in private to see if you would help me get one."

"Nina, that is a huge *ask*. I'm not against it because I believe it's a woman's right to choose what's best for her. But I do not want to overstep my boundaries by taking a minor to get something like that done without your parents knowing. Your dad at least."

"Well, you can forget them knowing. I almost feel like Nicole wants me to have this baby so that my life can be ruined. My dad head is so far up her ass; I don't think he can think for himself. Dylan's ass can go straight to hell. I've barely heard from him since all of this went down and I am still curious and baffled about his behavior."

"Speaking of Dylan. Remember in the hospital when you told me about that program, he said he was in that was covering his college tuition?"

"Yeah, what's the deal with that? Did you find out who sponsored him?"

"Everyone who I spoke with said there is no such program. They wish they could sponsor a kid for four years but the most they can offer is one-thousand-dollar scholarships."

"Oh really?"

"Yes. are you sure you got the program's name, right?"

"Yes, I'm positive."

"I'm not sure what's going on with him unless he has another girl and just didn't want to tell me."

"Wasn't he happy about the baby?"

"That's what his mouth says, but that is not what his actions show. I don't think he was truly happy about being a teenage dad and I'm damn sure not happy about being a teenage mom."

There were so many items to sift through and I had no idea where to start. It overwhelmed me looking around.

"Nina, you can start out married with kids and end up divorced and a single mom like my mother did. She struggled to raise me and my sibling because she was a housewife dedicated to her family and was blindsided by a divorce. My best friend's parents never married to this day when I visit their house it's filled with love and they have been together almost 30 years. There is no right or wrong way, Nina, ever body's journey is different." My eyes fluttered and I felt a rush of tears threatened to fall.

"Those are scenarios that I never thought of but your right. Bryce, this is just so much for me to deal with." The levee broke, and I wept. I couldn't hold my tears and my eyes were already sore from all the crying from the past week.

"It's okay, Nina, come here." Bryce stepped over boxes and embraced me.

"I should kick my own ass right now," Bryce said. I lifted my head from her chest, took a step back, and looked up at her.

"Why?"

"Because I never once thought of asking you if you were on birth control and that would've given you double protection."

"Please don't blame yourself, Bryce. I'm not dumb and I know having sex comes with risks. I just need to figure out what I'm going to do." Bryce sighed hard and gave me one more tight squeeze before she let go.

"Well, if it makes you feel any better, I can assure you this baby is going to be beautiful because you picked a fine ass little cutie to get fresh with." Bryce and I burst out laughing. It felt freeing to let go for a small moment.

"Bryce, that does not make me feel any better!" I yelled, throwing my head back and smiling through my wet eyes.

"How about going through some of your mommy's boxes. That should make you feel better." Bryce gave me three quick kisses on my forehead, while rubbing my arms.

"Now that WILL make me feel better."

"Do you want to start in these boxes over here?" Bryce was already making her way to the boxes labeled: picture frames.

"You can start there and see what you find. I'm going to start with this box that's not labeled and see what's in here." Opening the box gently, I removed the clear packing tape with my fingernails. I fell back.

"Oh my God! Oh my God!" My chest tightened, and my heart was beating a mile a minute. I saw Bryce drop some letters and run over.

"Nina, what's wrong?"

"What does that look like to you in that box?"

"Let me see." Scrambling to lift the flaps, Bryce hands shook. After carefully looking inside of the box, Bryce grabbed the sides of a beautiful urn.

"Nina, this looks like an urn. Do you think this is your mother's ashes?"

"I know it's my mother's ashes. I picked the urn myself. Nicole told me it got destroyed when the moving truck got into accident while moving my things here! That lying bitch. Bryce, I told you that she was pure evil!"

"Nina, why would she lie and create a story so horrible?"

"I have no idea, but I remember that being one of the worst

days of my life. I felt like I lost my mother all over again when she told me her urn was destroyed." I didn't realize I was now crying like a baby.

"Come here, sweetheart. That was an awful thing for Nicole to do to you. I don't understand why she would do anything like that." Bryce hugged me then let go and started rubbing her hands across the embossed engraving with her middle fingers. Bryce spoke gently.

"Omalara Fondula Ayinde. What a beautiful name for a beautiful woman."

"Thank you," I whispered.

"I feel like I just got my mom back."

"You did, Nina, and we will honor her properly. Your mom shouldn't be in a storage space. She deserves better than that."

"She does and I will make sure she gets better. Bryce, please help me get out of that house."

"Nina, I will do what I can to help you as best as I can, baby girl."

I wiped my nose and kissed my mother's urn. I was so happy and angry at the same time.

Chapter Thirty-four

The summer ended and I spent it with my Greats without visiting the family home once. My dad came over and visited with me a few times, but I avoided him as much as possible in fear of saying something extremely disrespectful that I wouldn't be able to take back. The thing that hurt most was missing out on all the volleyball camps I worked so hard to get into. I didn't attend the STEM camp at Tuskegee neither because going to school in Alabama was now off the table.

I spent most of the summer sick and my Greats thought it would be best to stay under a watchful eye. I was going through something I never experienced before and being away from home for two weeks scared me. I stayed with the people who showed me love and Bryce helped me refocus and reevaluate my future goals.

Since going through my mom's things and looking at her pictures, I decided that maybe I would keep this baby. It was a part of her and anything that was a part of Omalara Folade Ayinde I wanted to treasure. Bryce taught me how to start my mornings by meditating and journaling, which I found had a positive impact to my mental health.

When I pulled up to my father's house, I braced myself and was ready for whatever waited for me behind those doors.

"Glad to have you back home, Nina." I gave Maria a long hug; she was the only person I missed genuinely besides Greyson. While everyone in the home claimed they loved her, but worked her to the bone, I loved her because she made me feel seen and heard.

It felt weird walking into my room after being gone two months. I felt like the only space I had to myself was violated. My closet turned nursery was the worst part. Having my mom's urn back in my possession made up for my defaced mural a little bit. Now, I had to figure out a way to hide my mother's urn without risking Nicole hiding it from me again. The phone rang, breaking me out of my thoughts.

"Hello."

"Hey, Nina, how's things going? I wanted to check in on you now that you are back home." Bryce was concerned about my mental health. I told her I was fine repeatedly.

"Things are going okay. No one was here when my Greats

dropped me off except Maria Not one welcome home from the family."

"Maybe that's a good thing. That gives you time to get settled in peace. How's the baby?"

"That's true. The baby is fine. Hey, Bryce, I have to go, that's my dad beeping in." We ended the call.

"Hey, Dad."

"Hey, Nina. Pops told me that you came home. You settle in okay?"

"Yes. Where are you?"

"We took Nicole out for a quick birthday lunch. If I would've known you were coming home this early, we would've waited for you." I rolled my eyes. I wanted to end the call.

"That's okay. Enjoy the birthday lunch. I'm unpacking my things."

"We can come by and pick you up."

"No, I'm fine." The last thing I wanted to do was celebrate Nicole.

"Okay. After this, we have a couple more errands to run to finalize Nicole's party this weekend." My dad's enthusiasm sickened me.

"I'm going to transfer some money into your account so that Maria can take you shopping, and you can buy her a nice gift. I think with all that you guys have been through it would be a nice peace offering. I also want you to find something pretty to wear. It's going to be a themed party and the family is wearing all black."

"Okay, so the theme is death?" I was shaking my foot vigorously while biting my bottom lip. It was taking a lot of restraint not to mention my mother's urn.

"No, silly. It's a black attire only party." My insult went over my dad's head.

"Oh okay." I chuckled at my own joke.

"Can I invite a friend?"

"Sure, the more the merrier. Nicole spared no expense on her birthday party, and we're expecting a large amount of people so one more won't hurt."

"Okay. Bye Daddy.

"Bye baby and I am honestly happy you are back home. You belong with us. Not with your great-grandparents. I didn't respond. My father's mouth always said words that his actions didn't back up.

The next couple of days was a circus of landscapers, caterers, decorators, and photographers. I went unnoticed at home because everyone was making such a huge fuss about Nicole's birthday party. It was the talk of the town and I dreaded attending. Someone knocked on my bedroom door.

"Come in!" I yelled as I was laying across my bed, writing in my journal.

"Hey lady." I jumped up and hugged Bryce.

"What are you doing here?"

"Two special people that I love like they are my grandparents wanted me to come check on you. They seem to think young folks relate to young folks and asked me to make sure things were well here." I burst out laughing at the dramatics of Bryce. She moved her head from left to right, talking with exaggerated hand motions.

"I love the way you threw up air quotes when you said young folks relate to young folks. That sounds like something they would say for sure."

"Gotta love them. I sure wish I still had my great grandparents. You are blessed, Nina."

"I know, they are two awesome people."

"So real talk, how you feeling?"

"I feel okay. I still can't believe I'm pregnant and honestly other than sleepy I feel no real change."

"You still aren't showing. You don't look pregnant at all."

"I know but I'm sure I will get as big as a house eventually. It's still early."

"What about Dylan? Any word from him?"

"Not really. An occasional text here and there."

"Wow."

"How's things with your siblings?"

"The only one I like is the boy. Ryan and Riley are okay, I guess. Other than surface conversation, we don't really talk much. I guess they still mad I jumped on their mom. Nicole don't say shit to me. I know she hates that I am here. When she does speak it's forced. I try to avoid her because I still want to know why she had my mother's urn in a storage facility. That's really fucking with me, Bryce, so I try to stay away from her to prevent giving her another beatdown. I don't want any more confrontations. I just want to finish school so that I can leave.

"Where will you go? You are going to be a teenage mother. Whether you like it or not you are going to need support." Bryce plopped down on the bed beside me.

"Support is not something I have here. Other than financial support it's like I'm not a part of this family."

"Nina, do you think you tried to fit in?" I snapped my neck toward Bryce and slanted my eyes at her.

"I'm just playing devil's advocate in order to make you see all sides of a situation. You know how I do," she said with her palms in the air.

"I guess I have always felt unwanted from the very beginning, which made it hard for me to keep trying."

"I know abruptly coming here due to the tragic death of your mom was hard. I just wonder if you expected the same love that your mom poured into you from your stepmother."

"No...I honestly didn't have any high expectations for my stepmother, but I did expect so much more from my father. I'm unsure why. I just did."

"I will keep advising that you sit down and talk to him

about that."

"I've tried. When I do tell him, I want to talk to him he always finds a way to rope Nicole in. I feel like he can never address me one on one."

"Maybe him and his wife wants it to be a united front." Bryce laid across the bed.

"Maybe his wife wants to make sure we're not close."

"That's crazy. A wife and a daughter are two completely different relationships. I would think she wanted him to have a great relationship with his children." Bryce was leaning her face into the palm of her hand.

"Yeah, she does...with THEIR children, but his outside child...not so much."

"What a shame."

"Yes, it is. Are you coming to her birthday party this weekend?"

"Nope. Why would I want to come? I don't care for your stepmother at all." We burst out laughing.

"But yet and still you trying to convince me to love her. However, my dad said I could invite who I wanted, and I choose you. I don't want to have to stomach this party alone and I know my dad is not going to let me sit in my room all day."

"Ugh! I will swing by for a moment." Leaning into Bryce, I rubbed my cheek against hers.

"Yay, thank you and if nothing else the food will be amazing. One thing about Nicole, whether I like her or not, is that she knows how to spend my dad's money and throw lavish parties. She's a show-off and loves attention so it will be a fantastic party."

"What should I wear?"

"Where black. It's a formal party, darling." I was mimicking Nicole when I said that.

"Okay. I do have plenty of black in my closet."

Chapter Thirty-five

There was hustle and bustle everywhere downstairs. I had never seen so much fuss over a party. A huge photo of Nicole hung over the fireplace, replacing her family photo. Massive vases filled with red roses littered the room and the foyer had a huge waterfall placed on top of the large, circular marble table that normally held everyone's keys.

Tonight, was Nicole's night which was no different from any other night. Humble was not a word in her vocabulary. She proved that she was very much in love with herself and undoubtingly it seemed that everyone that knew her was in love with *her* as well. I was the minority. I saw through her flawless foolishness and could do without her.

"Nina, do you have your gown?" I looked up at Riley.

"What gown?"

"My mom got everyone custom gowns for the party tonight. Maria should have delivered it to your room."

"Wait, so we have to wear the same dresses? What if I didn't want to wear a gown?"

"Nina, these past couple of years you have been with us you still don't get it do you? It is not what you want to wear but what Mommy wants us to wear. This is her party and she meticulously planned out a theme." Riley rolled her eyes with her hands on her hips.

"But your mom throws parties all the time. What makes this one any different?"

"Duh, it's her 40th birthday party. This one is special, and we have to look the part." Riley was pointing her finger a little too close to my nose.

"Hmm okay."

Riley left and I walked toward my room. I honestly could care less about looking the part. That was this family's problem. Everyone looked the part, but no one cared sincerely about me, so I was no longer interested in pretending I was a wanted member of this family.

"Nina, I placed something in your closet!" Maria yelled at me from behind, startling me.

"Thank you, Maria," I said, smiling at her.

Walking into my room, I headed straight for my closet. I saw a large dress bag. I unzipped it and revealed the ugliest dress I had ever seen. It was all-black with ruffles and flared out under my breasts.

"Do you like it?"

Why is she always in my room and walking up on me like a sneaky thief? I used my right to remain silent and stared at her.

"I felt it was the best fit for your body since you're with child."

"I am not even showing yet, Nicole." I tried to shield my body and crossed my arms under my breasts.

"Your stomach may not be big but it's showing in all other areas of your body." Nicole twirled her finger from the top of my head all the way down to my bare feet. She loved fucking with my head. I felt like crumbling.

"Your shoes and stockings are in the bottom of the garment bag. Be ready and downstairs by six sharp! We're taking a family photo and your father insist you be in it."

She walked away and snapped her fingers. I rolled my eyes at her back. I reached down into the garment bag and pulled out a pair of black patent leather shoes. I liked the shoes but not as a match to the dress.

I sat on the floor of my closet to meticulously wrap my gift for Nicole. I knew it would take her breath away and I wanted it to be perfect.

I jumped up and looked around when I heard a knock. I was still on the floor of my closet where I dozed off.

"Come in!" I yelled. Riley and Ryan walked in wearing beautiful, sleek, black gowns. They looked like models. Riley had her long hair pinned up with curls pouring down the sides of her face and Ryan had her hair bone straight with a part in the middle.

"You guys look beautiful," I said as I got up off the floor.

"Nina, you're not ready? We are supposed to be dressed and downstairs for our family photo in five minutes." Ryan rolled her eyes and crossed her arms, displaying manicured finger French tips.

"Go without me. I fell asleep on the floor while wrapping your mother's present. This baby has me so tired all the time. Tell your mom that I will shower and get dressed as fast as I can."

"Well, hopefully, they will not be too upset. Lucky for you, they can't yell and scream at you about being tired all the time. You are with child," Ryan said, pointing at my stomach.

"I hope not. Take the family photo. I know my dad may be upset but I don't mind if I am not in it. I don't want to hold up Nicole's party. I know she has planned everything to a tee, and I don't want to ruin any of it for her."

Riley and Ryan left, and I let out a deep sigh. After seeing them, I already knew I was not wearing my hideous gown. Nicole made sure her girls were always shown in the best light possible and me in the worst. I jumped in the shower and took my time moisturizing my body and preparing for this dreadful party.

One hour later, I walked downstairs with a huge gift box in my hand and placed it on the gift table. The house was packed with people. It looked like a fancy funeral with everyone wearing all-black. I noticed Nicole wore a glamourous red, beaded gown with a small train. Her pale skin along with the flower in the side of her hair made her look like an old Hollywood movie star in the 1950s. Her race was ambiguous, and it was hard to tell if she was black or white.

"Nina." I turned around and it was Bryce. I was happy to see her.

"Hey, Bryce. You look beautiful." I hugged her and was greeted with a sweet floral scent.

Bryce had on an elegant black gown that was heart shaped in the front and dipped down dangerously low in the back. She had a slender diamond chain that dropped down the crease of her back and disappeared into the bottom of her dress. I wondered if it went in between her butt cheeks. I shuttered because if it did, I imagined that was uncomfortable.

"You look stunning, although I didn't think you would be dressed so differently from the rest?" Bryce stated.

"Wait until I show you the dress that was purchased for me is. Let's say it's undesirable so I had to wing it."

"And how did that go over with the step-monster?" Bryce asked with raised eyebrows.

"I haven't seen her yet."

"Well, get ready because she just spotted us, and she is walking in record speed over here to where we are."

"Nina! What are you wearing?"

Nicole tone was sharp, and her face flushed. She looked like a white woman who held her breath for too long. I ignored her question.

"Hey, Nicole. Nice party." I smiled and blinked, giving her a blank stare.

"What the hell are you wearing?" she demanded, but this time louder. People started to stare. My dad walked toward us, and Nicole grabbed my arm.

"Ouch!" I yelled dramatically, while grimacing in fake pain. If Nicole wanted to make a scene, I would perform for her.

"Take your hands off her, Nicole. You know she's in a delicate state why would you yank her up like that?" Bryce said.

"Who the hell are you?" Nicole hissed with both hands on her hips.

"Hey guys. What's going on over here?" my dad questioned.

"Hey Dad. I just got downstairs, and Nicole grabbed my arm." I rubbed my arm for emphasis.

"Look at her, Santino. This is not the dress I picked out for her to wear."

"I couldn't fit that dress, Nicole. I had to find something else."

My eyes watered and my Grandma Sabrina walked up fast,

holding the right side of her gown in her hands so she wouldn't step on it with her three-inch heels. A small crowd formed and before I knew it, my Greats burst through the crowd. My Grandpa Mario scooted his cane from left to right to move people out his way so he could see what was happening.

"Nicole, get a hold of yourself. It's just a dress. You're making a scene at your own party," my Grandma Sabrina said to her with disgust in her eyes.

"You will not be in any of my pictures, Nina." Nicole stared blankly. She walked away and switched like the brat she was.

"Okay," I said in a curt tone, while hunching my shoulders.

My all-white, off the shoulder dress made the statement I wanted it to make. It had a runched mid-section with a rhinestone cluster on the side. My hair had grown, and I had it pulled up in a massive twist out that poured out of a thick white head wrap. Since Nicole treated me like an outcast, I would dress like one.

"Whoa…that was intense," Bryce stated with wide eyes. She shook her head and looked back at Nicole mingling with her guests.

"That was unnecessary," my Grandma Sabrina said. "I can't believe that child snatched you up like that. She must have lost her mind. You okay, baby?"

"I'm okay."

"Nina, you knew that Nicole wanted us in all-black. Why would you wear white?" my dad asked with his arms folded. He was leaning into me like he was listening closely to whatever answer I was about to give him.

"Dad, did you see my dress?"

"No. Why?"

"Umm okay. Well, it didn't fit me."

"You didn't have anything else you could have worn?" My dad was rubbing his goatee.

"I could have worn my red dress, but I figured that wouldn't have gone over well," I said, looking over his shoulder at his wife.

"True. I guess you made the right choice then." My dad looked over his shoulder, then back at me, and gave me a dry peck on my forehead. He walked away to find his wife and try to soothe her bruised ego, I was sure.

Bryce snickered before stopping a waiter to get a lobster roll.

"Well, there is two things you got to admit," Bryce said as we walked and maneuvered inside of the massive family room.

"What's that?"

"This food is amazing, and your step-monster does look fabulous. I love that necklace she's wearing."

"Yeah...one thing Nicole knows how to do is be fashionable."

"There must be over a hundred people here."

"I think she is expecting one hundred-fifty guest."

"It's like a wedding."

"Or a funeral," I said, snickering.

Chapter Thirty-six

Bryce, my Uncle Legend, and I were chatting and stuffing our faces with food. I felt like my uncle was crushing on Bryce because he was not acting like his normal cocky self. He was laughing at everything Bryce said and grinning from ear to ear. Interrupting our free-flowing conversation, Nicole tapped on her wine glass with a spoon, gathering everyone to say a speech.

"Thank you everyone for attending my 40th birthday soiree." Cheers and claps erupted like she said something profound. I nudged Bryce and she nodded her head to the left, signaling for me to look over in that direction.

"Dylan? What is he doing here?" I whispered.

"No idea but I spotted him talking with Riley and Ryan a few seconds ago," Bryce whispered back.

"Every single one of you hold a special place in my heart, and I am grateful that you all are sharing in this moment with me. I want to thank my wonderful husband for throwing me this amazing party and I want to thank my babies Ryan, Riley, and Greyson. They are the apple of my eye."

I was disgusted and turned my head away. I guess her stepdaughter had no place in her heart. Glancing over at my dad, I wanted to see if he flinched when she said that. He didn't. Obviously, there was no room in his heart for his first daughter neither.

"Thank you for all the beautiful gifts. I see the table is flowing with presents." Nicole was behaving like a child trapped in a woman's body, flapping her hands like a seal.

"I will be opening gifts shortly but until then please enjoy the food, the wine, and each other."

"What adult says she will be opening gifts shortly? That's weird," Bryce stated.

"Typical Nicole behavior, honey. She's a showoff and will probably rank her gifts."

"She wouldn't," Bryce said, clutching imaginary pearls.

"I don't put anything past her. I cannot wait for her to open mine."

"Wait, you got her a gift? What is it?" Bryce asked with raised brows.

"You'll see." I smiled. I clasped my hands and tapped my pointer fingers together.

"Umm okay. What are you going to do about Dylan?"

"That, I'm unsure of. I haven't talked to him much in the past few weeks and I'm still confused by his behavior. I guess when you think you know someone maybe you don't. He's nothing like I thought he was. He completely fooled me and made a fool of me. I thought he was the one person around here that loved me."

"Well, little sister, it happens to the best of us. That's a man for you. They are complete assholes and since Dylan is still young, I would say he's a asshole in training who is mastering the asshole craft." I giggled but my Uncle Legend stiffened and smirked, looking sideways at the back of Bryce's head. He threw his hands up and pointed at her back. I covered my mouth to stop my laugh. Tapping on a glass, Nicole was getting everyone's attention again.

"Everyone, let's make our way to the foyer while I open my presents."

My dad took her hand and walked her up the steps to a high back chair on what looked like a small square stage. The chair was trimmed in gold with red, tufted velvet backing. It made it look like Nicole was sitting on a throne while her kids carefully placed her gifts at her feet.

"Open this one first, Mom," Riley squealed. "It's from me

and Ryan."

Nicole opened the blue Tiffany box and pulled out a bracelet. Smiling from ear to ear, she hugged her girls and squealed with delight.

"Thank you, my beautiful babies."

"I guess you weren't in on that gift, huh?" Bryce chuckled.

"I guess not," I responded dryly, not taking my eyes off this show. I looked at my dad, who was smiling like a Cheshire cat. I wondered how in the world he didn't see something wrong with this picture. He had to give them money to buy the gift. They didn't work to be able to afford jewelry like that.

"This one next, Mommy. It's from Grandma Sabrina and Grandpa Richard."

"Okay, let's have at it."

Nicole ripped open the packaging and found a bottle of fine wine.

"It's my favorite. Thank you, Mom and Dad!"

"It's the fakeness for me," I whispered to Bryce.

"Now this one, Mommy." Riley handed Nicole my gift.

"Who is this one from?" Nicole questioned.

"Let me check." Looking around, Riley couldn't figure out what my note attached said because she couldn't read cursive writing. They didn't teach it in school, and it was obvious her mom didn't teach her like my mother taught me, so she stood there stuck on stupid.

"Read the note, baby," Nicole said, baffled at her struggle.

"I can't," Riley whispered.

"Give it to me, child." Nicole took the note, pissed at the embarrassment.

"This one is from Nina?" Nicole frowned in disbelief. I guess she was surprised I gave her a beautifully wrapped gift. It was another thing my mom taught me; the beauty of wrapping a gift and making it look special.

"Yes, that gift is from me," I stated proudly, stepping up to the side of her make-shift stage.

"Wow. This is a surprise. Wherever you purchased this from they did a gorgeous job wrapping it."

The crowd agreed, murmuring how lovely it was.

"I wrapped it myself," I said in an elevated tone.

"Sure, you did. Well, let me open it." She forced a smile and nodded her head like I was lying. She untied the bow.

"Be careful. It's fragile and priceless," I said as she opened the huge box.

When Nicole opened the lid, her face turned beet red.

"What is it?" someone yelled out.

"Pull it out and show us," another one of her guests yelled.

"I'll help you, baby." My dad walked beside her and carefully pulled out the crafted beauty.

"What in the hell is this!" my dad yelled.

"You don't recognize it, Daddy?"

"It's my mother's urn!" I yelled. All I heard were gasps and Nicole looked like she stopped breathing.

Chapter Thirty-seven

"Nicole, I thought this was destroyed in the move here? Why in the hell would you lie about that? Where has it been all this time?" My dad's eyes were cold as he stared at her, waiting for an answer. His nostrils flared and I swore steam were coming out of his ears.

"It was in the storage unit hidden away in some boxes. I found it by accident." I decided to answer since Nicole was mute.

"What were you doing in my storage unit? I didn't give you permission to go through my things in storage!" Nicole was yelling to the top of her lungs, ignoring my father's question.

"It's not your storage unit, Nicole. That storage unit is ours for things that we have no space for in this house. It wasn't for hiding something as important as Nina mother's ashes! What the hell is wrong with you? Why would you lie and say this was destroyed?" My dad's voice cracked which surprised me.

The silence was so pronounced, you could hear a pin drop while everyone waited for Nicole to answer my father. I walked toward Nicole's makeshift stage and grabbed my mother's urn then made my way back toward Bryce. I wanted to put my mother in my room or somewhere safe before she turned up missing again.

"Get out! Everybody get out!" Nicole shouted out of nowhere.

"Maria, you and the rest of the staff get everyone out of my house." Nicole pointed to the door.

My dad's chest was rising and falling at a rapid speed. I was beginning to get a little nervous because I never saw my dad so angry. He walked to Nicole, grabbed her arm, and snatched her from the stage.

Nicole's heels were loud as she stammered down the stage, she appeared sloppy drunk or lightheaded. I knew her acting was about to kick into an Oscar worthy performance. Nicole cried and heaved like she was in excruciating pain. I felt a hand on my shoulder and turned to see Dylan looking at me with tormented eyes.

"Nina, I'm sorry," he said, barely audible. My uncle was on his ass like gravy on rice. He snatched him up by his neck, rushed him to the nearest wall, and slammed his head with a force so hard that I thought it would leave a dent in the wall.

"Legend, stop, stop, stop! Let him down!" Bryce yelled

forcefully, while rubbing my uncle's arm to ease his anger. A small part of me wanted him to choke Dylan the fuck out.

"Give me one good reason why I should let this fool down," my uncle growled through gritted teeth.

"He's the father of Nina's baby. He's young and dumb. He deserves to give Nina some answers. Let him down, Legend, please." Bryce words were so soothing, my uncle dropped Dylan, leaving him gasping for air.

"You lucky you fine as fuck or I will have killed his little ass," my Uncle Legend said in a harsh whisper, pointing his finger close to Bryce's face. Bryce looked unbothered. She grabbed his hand and kissed the back of it.

"Nina, I think it would be a great time for you and Dylan to talk." My heart raced. I spent months thinking about what I would say to him but in this very moment I was speechless. I had a million questions but couldn't find my voice to ask any one of them.

"Nina, maybe you can find a quiet corner or go upstairs so you can have some privacy," Bryce said, snapping me out of my trance.

"Nah, let this little asshole say what he has to say right here where I can hear him. Nigga, start talking before I punch you in the fucking throat!" My Uncle Legend was seething.

"Legend, why don't you take me to get a drink from the bar. I'm hungry too so let's grab some of this food to eat." Bryce pulled him by his arm.

When his strong ass didn't bulge, she stepped in front of him and wrapped her arms inside of his suit jacket, walking him toward the dining area. The house was in a state of commotion and all I heard was yelling and questions thrown at Nicole from my dad, my greats, and my grands. I felt no pity for her. I prayed they chewed her up and spit her out.

"Can we talk?" Dylan was rubbing his throat, which had red bruises forming.

"Sure, let's go upstairs so I can put my mother's urn somewhere safe, or are you going to report that to Nicole too?" I rolled my eyes and made my way upstairs while he followed me with his head hung low and his hands in his pockets.

When I got upstairs to my room, I decided I was not going to hide my mother's urn. I sat it on full display on the top of my dresser. My mother didn't deserve to be hidden; I wanted to see her every day the moment my eyes opened. Now that everyone knew what Nicole did, I dared her to step foot in my room and touch her urn again.

"It's beautiful right there," Dylan said. I whipped my head around almost forgetting that he was in my room. I rolled my eyes and stared at him so harsh that eventually he turned his head and rubbed the back of his neck.

"So how have you been feeling, BK?"

"I've been feeling like shit, Dylan. I've been sick the whole summer, I lost my college volleyball opportunities. I couldn't attend STEM camp and I will be entering my senior year pregnant. All while you live out your dreams at Morehouse. That's how I've been feeling. How is it my life changed drastically and yours didn't?"

"Nina, I didn't think any of this would go down like this."

"Oh really? What did you think would happen? What did think betraying Nina would look like? A walk in the park? Me and Nicole walking hand in hand into the sunset. You fucking fake ass, you knew Nicole was putting me through hell. I told you that shit time and time again and you pretended that you cared, let me cry on your shoulder and everything while walking me into the pits of hell." I had to pause for a moment and catch my breath. This baby had me winded.

"Why would you tell Nicole and my dad I was pregnant, knowing that I didn't want this baby?"

Dylan approached me, trying to wrap his arms around me, but I pushed him away. Dylan grabbed me and placed me against the wall with his arms on both sides of it forcing me into his makeshift prison. I smelled the Versace cologne that I bought him last Christmas blanket his skin. I looked up and tears fell from his eyes.

"BK, she promised me a future. One that was unattainable for me in my world. She promised to pay my tuition at Morehouse, and she's already taken care of the first year. Nicole told me that you would be well cared for and that they would make sure you had a full-time nanny so that you could still go to college."

"What?" I whispered.

"They... My father too?"

"No, no, not your dad. Not that I know of. I only spoke with Mrs. Nicole."

I slid down onto the floor and Dylan slid down next to me.

"Why would she want to ruin my life?"

"Nina, she told me because you ruined hers." I gasped for air. I was more confused than ever because I never once did anything to Nicole except exist.

"Nina, I was so against it. I told her no, that I couldn't do that to you. She then went to my mom and told her that she would pay for her to finish school so that she could go from being a LPN to a RN. Dangling that salary difference in my mom's face had her put more pressure on me to go through with Nicole's plan."

"Dylan," I cried out. I felt a pain that was indescribable. It felt like someone ripped me apart from the inside.

"That means that all the times you told me you cared about me was a lie. You're a liar!"

"Nina, have you ever been hungry? Have you ever spilt a pack of oodles and noodles with your mom because that was all you had until her next payday? Have you ever had to miss school because you had to go to work because your mother depended on you to help her make ends meet? I have and it clouded my judgement. You have a home...I mean, it's not perfect here but look at how you live. Your family has a driver and live-in help. I always assumed that you were exaggerating and emotional because of your mother's death. It wasn't until tonight when I saw your mother's urn turn up, that I knew that I made a horrific decision trusting Nicole. Nina, I'm so sorry." I stood to my feet and smoothed out my gown.

"I'd rather struggle with a mother that loves me than live this life that I have that you think is so wonderful. Get out of my room." Dylan slowly got off the floor and went toward my door.

"Dylan," I called out. He turned around with hopeful eyes.

"Yeah, BK?"

"I'm not exaggerating when I tell you that I am going to go downstairs and tell my Uncle Legend everything that you just told me. I want to see how emotional you get when that loose cannon fucks you all the way up!" Dylan's eyes widened, and he skedaddled out of my room. I laid across my bed and cried.

Chapter Thirty-eight

I laid in my bed, saturating my pillow with tears. I couldn't describe the pain I was feeling. I was hurting all over and the sharpest pain was in my heart. The shock and hurt from Dylan's behavior showed me how mean the world could be to me. The rage inside of me snuffed out with the feelings of disbelief. I grinded my teeth as I laid still, trying to process what just happened. My door opened with Bryce and my Uncle Legend walking in.

"Hey, sweetheart, I noticed Dylan slither out the front door with haste which leads me to believe things didn't go so well," Bryce stated.

"It didn't," I responded in defeat.

"I blame you, Bryce. You should've let me choke his ass

out while I had the chance," My Uncle Legend said, rolling his eyes at Bryce.

"Shut up," Bryce said, waving her hand in front of my uncle's face.

"Nina, come on, baby. Let's try to eat something. You have a life inside of you depending on you for nourishment." Bryce and my uncle pulled me up to a sitting position.

"I'm not hungry," I sulked.

"Well, come downstairs and watch me eat again." My Uncle Legend smiled, which lifted my spirits and got me up.

There was still some commotion and arguing going on when we got downstairs. It was maybe ten to fifteen people left in the house. My dad was going at it with Nicole. My Greats were asking her questions and looking at her with disdain while my grands waited for answers. I thought my Grandma Sabrina was going to slap fire from her. She tapped her foot on the floor a mile a minute and she was scarlet red with anger.

The bell rang again, and Maria rushed to open the door, wiping her hands down her black and white uniform. I lost my breath when she opened the door. I felt a sharp pain in my stomach. My mind was playing tricks on me. Blinking a hundred miles per minute, I looked up at the door again and it was my uma and umpa. I felt lightheaded and stumbled.

"Whoa, are you okay, Nina?" Bryce asked, holding me up.

"Who are they?"

"Those are my mother's parents." I walked swiftly, while holding up my gown, and fell into my grandparents' arms.

"Uma. Umpa. What are you guys doing here. I'm so grateful to see you. It's been way too long."

"Yes, dear. We know. *Me do wo.* We've missed you deeply," my umpa's baritone voice boomed. My grandparents' embrace felt like a vice grip. I didn't want to let them go.

"What's all the commotion going on around here?"

"Uma, it would take me a lifetime to fill you in," I said with my head deep in her bosom.

"Well, baby, we don't have that long," she chuckled. Holding my face with her two soft hands, my uma looked into my eyes.

"Santina Omalara, your eyes tell me that you are troubled. We do not know what is going on, but something is. We have not heard back from you, and we have sent many attempts to reach you. deɛn nti?"

"You did?" I asked baffled.

"Aane. We called and wrote letters."

"I never got them, Uma. I thought you forgot about me."

"How could we forget about our only daughter's child?"

"Why didn't you come back and get me Uma? I wish you would've taken back with you to Ghana." My grandfather moved closer and placed his hands on my shoulders.

"We wish we could have too, but it was not that easy."

"Mr. and Mrs. Ayinde, it's good to see you." My dad came out of nowhere and hugged my grandparents. They didn't return the gesture.

"Please excuse all the commotion. Tonight, has been full of surprises. Please come in and make yourselves at home." My dad tried taking them into the family room, but they didn't budge.

"We would like to spend some private time with Nina. We need to talk to her about her inheritance that was left for her. Now that she will be eighteen in a few weeks she will be able to receive it."

"Inheritance? I didn't know she had an inheritance," my dad whispered with his attention elsewhere. Nicole with all the crying and speaking with my Grands was distracting him.

"You weren't supposed to. My daughter was very responsible and made sure when she turned of age, she would be financially secure and independent," my uma stated.

"She was responsible." My dad agreed, looking down at his shoes in shame. My grand-parents' presence made him uncomfortable. Suddenly, my uma was flustered. She held her hand over her mouth and let out a loud gasp.

"What's wrong, Mrs. Ayinde?" my dad asked.

She didn't answer. Instead, she walked straight into the room where Nicole stood with us on her heels. I wasn't sure what was happening. It was like my uma was possessed.

"You take that off right now, Nicole! How dare you!" She

quickened her pace and stood directly in front of Nicole. Nicole's eyes widened with fright.

Slap

My uma hit Nicole across her face so hard it turned red.

"Did you just strike me?" Nicole's eyes were wide with horror, and she held her face.

"Where did you get my daughter's necklace from? Omalara had that custom handmade for her in Africa during a visit home. That was supposed to be gifted to Nina when she turned eighteen. It represents royalty and it was to bring her good luck and protection against negative energy and evil spirits." My uma snatched the necklace off Nicole's neck, breaking it.

I watched the necklace fall to the ground. I picked it up and stared at it. It was beautiful. I admired it around Nicole's neck several times and all along it was mine.

"Tino, we're taking Nina to stay with us in our Airbnb for the next two weeks. We have a lot to talk to her about. We want to spend time with our grand-daughter." Umpa wasn't asking. His authoritative tone indicated he was letting my dad know.

"Sir, if it's okay I would like to take you guys out to dinner while you're here in America." My dad's hands were clasp behind his back, then he placed them in his pocket. He kept darting his head back at Nicole. My dad shook his head in disbelief.

"Santino, we will think about it. Right now, we are truly disappointed, and we just want to spend time with Nina. We'll be in touch. Nina, grab a bag, honey. Let's head out. Your uma and

I had a long day of travel, and we want to settle in."

I was over this party and this family. I grabbed Bryce to help me go upstairs and pack my bags. Finally, I was out of here.

One year later...

Standing at my granite island in the kitchen of my townhouse, I happily prepped dinner for Bryce and my Greats. It was a tough year. In November, I was in labor for five hours, but the baby was still born. I pressed the button for the drugs non-stop. It didn't make sense to feel all that pain with no bundle of joy at the end. It was a girl, and I named her Sun. I honored her with a small memorial in the hospital's chapel. I didn't contact Dylan because it was still too painful to see him, but my dad let him know. Whenever I felt depressed or sad, I looked up in the sky and imagined that my mother was holding Sun. Rainbows, warm weather, and birds flying high always made me think of her and smile. It helped keep her memory alive.

"Nina, can you believe you are a homeowner, cooking in your own kitchen?" Bryce walked up to me and hugged me as I chopped tomatoes and red onions for our salad.

"Can you believe you're a freshman in college paying your own tuition?" My Grandma Diane said. "You were so smart to spend your inheritance on buying a home," she beamed.

"Not, a home," my Grandpa Mario chimed in. "Two homes!"

"Yes! Nina, I think we should toast to you. Buying a duplex and renting out one while you live in the other is genius. You are already ahead of your generation in so many ways." Bryce was beaming with pride. She was a good mentor to me.

"Thanks, guys. Honestly, I must give thanks to my mom. She loved me fiercely and always told me she would take care of me. She honored that in her life and in her death. I wish I didn't have to go through all that hell before I could receive it." I choked back tears as I glanced at her urn on my fireplace mantle.

"Baby, I know your transition into our family wasn't easy, and I know it was tough in that household with Nicole treating you so horribly. But all of that prepared you to be able to enjoy the blessing that you have today. If you would've gotten that inheritance earlier than you wouldn't have been able to responsibly appreciate what you have here."

"How's the therapy sessions going with your dad?" Bryce asked.

"It's going well. We are taking it really slow because I have so much built-up resentment in my heart toward him. He did apologize and tell me he was a coward. So, at least he has taken some accountability." I darted my eyes from side to side while chopping. I couldn't believe I was taking up for him.

"Part of our homework from the therapist is to spend the

weekend together getting to know each other deeper. We're driving up to the mountains this weekend and I'm nervous because he told me he's going to tell me how him and my mom met."

"Why are you nervous?" Bryce asked me.

"I'm not sure. But I did write down a list of questions and things I wanted to say to him in our therapy journal. We'll see how the weekend goes."

"Well, baby, we pray that you get some closure," my grandma said.

"I don't even think he realized half the stuff she was doing. You know how some people numb themselves with drugs and alcohol? I think your dad numbs himself with work. He always got excuses on why he spends so much time away from the home," my Grandpa Mario scoffed.

"I think he is going through the motions with her and those kids. He's a lump of flesh mindlessly moving in this world." My grandma sucked her teeth.

"Hmmm, you think Nicole has a spell on him. She is one of those Creoles from Louisiana, isn't she?" My grandpa blurted out. I chuckled.

"I don't know about that. However, what I learned is that I can't force someone to love me the way I feel that they should. My dad may never be able to love me the way my mother loved me. I don't think he knows how. At this point, I just take it one therapy session at a time. I am not even sure if Nicole knows that my father and I attend therapy twice a month. Last we spoke, he was still living in the guest house after what went down at her party."

"Changing gears. Dylan came by the community center to sign up for some volunteer hours. You know he's not at Morehouse any longer and enrolled into Eastern Community College," Bryce stated. My eyes swelled with tears.

"That's a chapter in my life that I have not gotten over. I wish Dylan well but finding out that he made a deal with Nicole to get me pregnant in return for her paying for his tuition at Morehouse is unforgivable," I sniffled.

"Yeah, that was pretty horrible. I think that woman may be the evilest person that I have ever come across. She was hell bent on ruining your life," Bryce sneered.

"She underestimated me. Although I lost my baby, had I had her, I would've never been Nicole. I still would've thrived because of the support I had from you two." I looked at my Greats with a lone tear falling on my cheek and then I turned and looked over at Bryce.

"And you, Bryce. You guys have supported me and held me up during some of my darkest days. You loved me when I needed it most. It took me realizing that instead of looking for love in a place where it was unavailable, for me to embrace the love in the places where it was being offered to me."

"Cheers!" Bryce yelled. Everyone held up their lemonade and clinked their glasses.

"Now, let's dig into this Sunday dinner. I'm glad you guys trust me because you know I'm still learning how to cook."

Everyone laughed when I revealed my dry meatloaf.

To be continued....

.

ALSO BY DELIA ROUSE

*Coming soon!
Flawless Foolishness 2: F^2

BY DELIA NICOLE

Wonders of a Woman
*available on DeliaRouse.com

ABOUT THE AUTHOR

To stay updated on all things Delia Rouse follow her on her social media platforms.

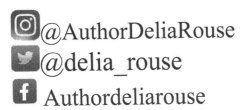

@AuthorDeliaRouse
@delia_rouse
Authordeliarouse

You can also join her Facebook group
Delia's Rouse's Desired Reads.

_____ORDER FORM

_____

INMATES ONLY receive novels for $10.00 per book PLUS shipping fee PER BOOK.
(Mail Order MUST come from inmate directly to receive discount)

_____	_____	$15.00
_____	_____	$15.00
_____	_____	$15.00
_____	_____	$15.00
_____	_____	$15.00
_____	_____	$15.00
_____	_____	$15.00
_____	_____	$15.00

Please add **$5.00 for shipping and handling fees for up to (2) BOOKS PER ORDER.**
(INMATES INCLUDED)

PUBLICATIONS ADDRESS: _____

CUSTOMER'S NAME: _____

ADDRESS: _____

CITY/STATE: _____

CONTACT/EMAIL: _____

Please Allow 8-10 Business Days Before Shipping

NOTE: Due to COVID-19 Some Orders May Take Up To 3 Weeks Before They Ship

We are NOT responsible for Prison Orders rejected

NO RETURNS and NO REFUNDS * NO PERSONAL CHECKS ACCEPTED*
STAMPS NO LONGER ACCEPTED